WICKED HUNTER

SAM WICK UNIVERSE THRILLER #6

CHASE AUSTIN

THRILLVERSE PUBLISHING

ABOUT WICKED HUNTER

Wick has just got the orders to free a CIA agent from the clutches of the Taliban. Only problem, the agent is captive at the heart of the Taliban fort.

It's a suicide mission but Wick has a choice. He can abandon the mission and let the agent die. A tight-rope moral balancing act with Sam Wick at the pivot point.

From Chase Austin, the sensational author of Wicked Deceit and Wicked Storm, comes another high-stakes thriller featuring the world's most dangerous assassin: Sam Wick. Expect the unexpected in this gritty, tense, and page-turning thriller from the sensational author Chase Austin. The Taliban has abducted a CIA agent. No one knows where he is being kept. Time is running out. Can he be saved?

CHAPTER 1

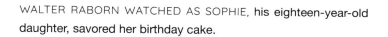 WALTER RABORN WATCHED AS SOPHIE, his eighteen-year-old daughter, savored her birthday cake.

"Dad, stop looking at me like that! You're making me self-conscious." She turned his face away with a cake-soiled hand.

Raborn grinned at her gesture. How soon kids grew up. He picked up a tissue to wipe his cheek.

"What next?" she asked, beaming.

"How about a movie? Raborn said.

"Dad, Gone with the Wind is not running in theaters anymore, and I don't want to spend the rest of the evening sitting in a cramped, smelly seat."

"So, you think the movie I watched last was Gone with the Wind?"

Sophie waved his indignation away. "I'm thinking along the lines of a vacation."

"Vacation?"

"Yes, it's been years since you, me and Mom went anywhere."

"Your Mom and I getting anywhere within fifty yards of each other is always a bad idea."

"Ah...Dad, you guys look so good together! If you ask me, you should give each other one more chance."

"Your mom and I are happy the way we are."

"I don't see you happy."

.   .   .

"Maybe because you don't see me very often."

"If you stayed with us, I would see you more often."

"I heard you're going back to Columbia next week," Raborn said, attempting to change the topic.

"I am, but I'm not going forever, am I? Dad, I hate having to shuttle between your place and Mom's, to see you both."

"I don't know, kiddo. Your mom and I separated on a bad note. Even our fond moments are colored with bitterness."

Raborn's tone had an unstated sadness that Sophie understood. So, it was she who changed the topic this time. "You spoke to Mr. Helms about my internship?" William Helms was the director of the NSA and arguably one of the most respected men in the intelligence community.

The expression on her father's face told her everything she needed to know. After a short pause, Raborn said, "I will ask him, but you still haven't told me why you want to do an internship at the NSA."

"I told you I'm considering a career as a cryptocurrency analyst. What better place than the NSA for someone like me after

Columbia?"

"I thought you were just trying to scare me off by choosing an agency like NSA."

"Dad, it's just a desk job, playing with the computer, nothing scary."

"Maybe." The real reason for Raborn's hesitation was NSA's lower billing against CIA, but he decided not to voice his opinion.

"The director of the CIA should not say such things."

"Why don't you come and see if something in the CIA interests you?"

"Dad, we have already discussed this."

"Okay, fine." Raborn raised his hand to signal for the check.

"Sir." The head of Raborn's security detail stepped up to the table, cell phone in hand. "Roy is on the line. He says it's urgent."

.   .   .

Raborn looked at him with a neutral expression and then checked his own cell. Three missed calls. He had put the phone on mute for the dinner date with his daughter.

"Tell Roy I'll call him," Raborn said.

Sophie noticed the sudden change in her father's tone. "Dad, everything alright?"

"Everything's fine. I just need to take this call." Raborn rose from his chair and went to a secluded corner before dialing Roy's secure line. Roy picked up before the second ring.

"Roy."

"Sir, this is about Josh Fletcher."

Raborn knew Josh Fletcher, an old CIA hand who was currently in Afghanistan, operating undercover as a CNN reporter, to track the Taliban's activities.

"I'm listening." Raborn maintained his composure.

"He has been incommunicado for the last five hours. We tracked the location of his commlink device to the Helmand Province, near the Afghanistan–Pakistan border. The location is deep in Taliban territory, so chances are that they might have got suspicious. We're already tracking any unusual movement at their known hideouts, but there's nothing noteworthy till now."

Raborn listened without interrupting. His ambition to carve out a successful political career in DC had just faced its first test, and he did not know how much damage the test would inflict before it would end. His mind raced.

"Which of our assets are nearest to Helmand? Check all databases, not only the CIA's," he instructed Roy.

"I already have the names of two operatives who can be mobilized quickly. There's Peter Adams of the CIA, and there's this guy called Sam Wick."

"Sam Wick?"

"Yes, sir." The recognition in Raborn's tone surprised Roy. The fact that his boss knew the name of a lowly field operative who wasn't a CIA asset was unusual.

Raborn nodded. He knew now what he had to do. "Connect me to William Helms in five minutes." He disconnected and returned to his table to bid Sophie goodbye.

CHAPTER 2

WILLIAM HELMS WAS at the dinner table. Martha, his wife of forty years sat on his left, and Chloe, his daughter, was to his right. But William's attention was on the midterm election debate raging on TV, that he was watching surreptitiously from the corner of his eye.

The panel featured three reporters and the special guest, Secretary of Defense Patrick Mattis, sitting in a semicircle, around a horseshoe news desk.

"Secretary Mattis, this week has been extremely difficult for the government here in the nation's capital… probably more so for you than most. President Hancock's proposed amendment to withdraw the American troops from Afghanistan, bringing a sudden end to a military campaign that largely vanquished the Taliban and ceding a strategically vital country to China and Russia, has not met with a positive response. Many political pundits, and of course the Democrats, have criticized the move, calling it immature. How do you see the events of the last several days and how will they affect the US president's approval ratings?"

Mattis shifted in his chair. "To call the last few days difficult is an understatement. But what most people don't understand is how certain decisions need to be made despite what popular opinion says. We hope that the Democrats will see reason and support our armed forces. President Hancock is a very strong leader, and under his able leadership we will move forward and get back to the business of governing this country."

Helms could clearly see how uncomfortable Mattis was on camera. Despite being a politician, he wasn't a very good liar, and this was clearly visible under studio lights. The truth was that not only had President Hancock overruled his generals and civilian advisers to fulfill his frequently expressed desire to bring home American forces from a messy foreign entanglement, but his decision, conveyed via his own social media handle on Wednesday, had plunged the administration's Afghanistan strategy into disarray, rattling allies like Britain and Israel, who were faithful partners in fighting the Taliban.

The abrupt, chaotic nature of the move—and the opposition it immediately provoked on Capitol Hill and beyond—raised questions about how the President would follow through with the full withdrawal. Even after the President's announcement, officials said, the Pentagon and State Department were still trying to talk him out of it.

.   .   .

Helms tried to stay calm, though the bridge of his nose crinkled with tension. He asked himself once again, "What in hell is he up to?"

"Bill, you're doing it again," Martha said, her disapproval evident in her tone. "Sometimes, it's better to switch off from what is happening around the world, and just enjoy the moment."

"I know, I know." He raised his hands in surrender.

Chloe picked up the remote and switched off the television, laughing. Helms gave her a look of mock anger but knew better than to protest. He turned his attention to the food.

"What's this for?" he asked, forking his steak.

"We're celebrating, Dad."

"Celebrating?"

"For your taking a day off in a decade," Martha said with a smile.

"I have taken days off now and then," Helms protested.

·   ·   ·

"Not under our watch," Chloe said, firmly.

Helms decided not to contest this claim and focused on the steak. It seemed juicy and tender.

"How is it?" Martha asked.

"A little different today but, like always, the best," Helms replied, dabbing his mouth with a tissue.

"It's Chloe who should get all the credit for this," Martha said.

"Really?" Helms was mildly surprised.

"I know it's not like how Mom makes it—"

"You are right, it's better." Helms cut in, making both the ladies chuckle.

They were halfway through their dinner when the phone rang. It was the secure line. Helms instinctively got up, avoiding Martha's gaze. She hated people leaving the table in the middle of the meal. But, as NSA director, he did not have the luxury of ignoring calls on the secure line that few people had access to.

This better be important, he thought grimly as he picked up the receiver, or the caller's toast.

"Helms speaking."

"Sir, Walter Raborn wants to talk to you," the operator chimed in.

"Patch him in," Helms said after a thoughtful pause. He knew Raborn, but a call at home from the director of the CIA was unusual, to say the least.

"Helms Speaking."

"Helms, do you know the whereabouts of Sam Wick?"

"Sam Wick?" Wick was the best asset of Task Force 77 or TF-77, currently stationed in Afghanistan. TF-77 was a team of highly skilled operatives. The team was overseen by the NSA and the US military and was equipped to handle anything. The team was capable to execute the toughest missions, penetrate the most dangerous locations, often through means that no government could overtly authorize. No one knew the exact size of this team or how many assets it had, except for a handful of individuals, which did not include even the President of the US. As its custodian, it was Helms' responsibility to protect this team from the diplomatic circus and that was why Raborn was on the phone with him.

·   ·   ·

"Yes, we have a problem at the Afghanistan–Pakistan border, and we need someone in the field who is an expert of that terrain. My sources mentioned that Sam is in the region."

"What kind of problem?" Helms asked, grimly. This wasn't the first time Raborn had maneuvered him into a position he would rather not have been in.

Raborn gave him a redacted version of the story.

The more Helms listened to Raborn the more his reservations about this untimely call grew. The story didn't seem convincing. The CIA had agents stationed in the same territory already, Helms knew, and yet they were asking for Sam. Even so, he kept his thoughts to himself as Raborn updated him on the situation. He listened patiently to Raborn's theories regarding the possible abduction but reserved judgment until he could cross-check them after the call. Instead, he assured Raborn that the inter-agency politics would not get in the way where an agent's life was concerned. He promised Raborn that he would have an appropriate response within a couple of hours.

Helms looked at Martha and Chloe who were waiting for him to return to the table. "Something's come up. I'll finish dinner in my office," he told them, picking up his plate and striding to his home office.

.   .   .

Martha and Chloe gazed after him, then turned back to their dinner. They had seen this too many times to take offense. And they knew whatever had come up must be of vital importance, if Helms was sacrificing his precious day off.

Helms closed the door of his home office and picked up his Blackberry. He scrolled to the name of Riley Miller—Wick's handler—and pressed the dial button. Three rings later an alert voice greeted him.

"Riley, I need to talk to Sam. How soon can you patch a secure connection?"

"It's 0600 hours in Afghanistan so Wick should be in the safe house. It should not take much time, sir," Riley said.

"Okay, call me on this number as soon as you get a hold on him."

CHAPTER 3

TF-77's Safe House, Afghanistan

Sam Wick had been lying on a bare cot, staring at the rotating ceiling fan for the last four hours. His eyelids were heavy, and he had a splitting headache but even so, he couldn't sleep. It wasn't as if he hadn't tried, but the naps never lasted more than fifteen-twenty minutes. Finally, he got up and ambled towards the kitchen, craving some black coffee.

The safe house was located in the Helmand province of Afghanistan and belonged to TF-77. Wick was one of the last draft picks from West Point for TF-77 and no one, not even Helms, who led the TF-77 along with the NSA, had imagined his meteoric rise in such a short time. He had been picked as the backup of the backup of the backup. That didn't mean he wasn't good, it simply meant there had been others in his batch who were far better than him when they first joined the TF-77, but over time Wick had doggedly emerged as TF-77's best asset.

His hit rate, hovering at ninety-five percent for the last five years, the best among the current crop of TF-77 assets, spoke of his tenacity.

At 5'11", his weather-beaten face had a rugged attraction, not least because of his unreadable sea-blue eyes, bright with intelligence. With his slicked-back black hair and athletic build, he seemed like a man on a mission. According to his file, he could speak seventeen languages with a neutral accent, including Arabic, Urdu, and Hindi. This made him an excellent choice for being deployed in countries like Afghanistan, Iraq, and Pakistan.

Till seven months ago, he had considered himself an orphan, but then during a mission in Poland, he had stumbled onto information about the identity of his parents and the possibility that they might still be alive. Since that day, he had been trying to find the missing pieces, but had so far been unsuccessful in finding anything substantial that he could latch on to.

The problem was that he wasn't completely certain if he wanted to find the people who had abandoned him ages ago. What would he do even if he found them? There wasn't any kind of emotional connect he felt with them anymore. There was curiosity maybe, but was that enough to invite further complications in his already troubled life?

Wick was about to sit back on his cot with his coffee mug when his comm beeped. He put down the mug on the side table and put on his headset. It was Riley, his handler.

Fifteen minutes later, Helms' phone rang. It was Riley, along with Wick.

"Thanks, Riley, you can drop off now," Helms said. It wasn't a request.

"Sure, sir." There was confusion in her voice. Helms ignored it. For what he wanted to discuss with Wick, he needed privacy. There was a click, and they both knew they were the only ones on the call.

"Who else is with you in the safe house?" Helms asked, without preamble.

"I'm alone."

Helms cleared his throat. "I got a call from Raborn." Helms let the gravity of the name sink in. "Josh Fletcher, a CIA operative in Afghanistan tracking the Taliban, was supposed to report at the CIA's Gereshk base to attend a debriefing session, a few hours ago. But he has not only missed it but has also gone radio silent. His last known location is near the Helmand province where you are right now. They want our help in finding him."

"Why us? The CIA must have enough operatives in the region?"

. . .

"Raborn needs someone who knows the terrain well. He has categorically asked for you." Helms then gave him a detailed summary of his conversation with Raborn. Wick listened with rapt attention.

"What's your opinion on the request?" he asked once Helms had filled him in.

"I don't have a good feeling about this," Helms shared his views.

Wick knew Helms would not say something like this without giving it proper thought. Helms had one of the sharpest minds in the intelligence community and he was the only person whose opinion Wick respected.

"How many assets do the CIA have in the region?" Wick asked.

"Anywhere between twenty to thirty," Helms said.

"Yet they come to us for a straightforward mission like this."

"That is precisely my problem."

. . .

"What about this missing asset, this Josh, what do we have on him?" Wick asked.

"I have already asked an analyst to look into him," Helms said. "His bank and telephone records, his family, everything connected to him. You will get a report soon."

"What does the CIA have on him? If he has been in the field for so long, then he must have routed a lot of intel to them."

"Raborn is sending a folder on him in thirty minutes."

"Did he mention how he wants this arrangement to move forward?"

"It looks like he wants us to lead this entirely," Helms replied.

"He wants it, or he asked for it?" Wick asked.

"From his tone, he wants it to happen."

"What about the Taliban hideouts in that region?"

.   .   .

"Our database shows six known hideouts near the Helmand province. The CIA is also surveilling them but nothing unusual has been noted as of now."

"How sure are they it's the Taliban and not ISIS?"

"Raborn seemed pretty sure."

"What if Josh has gone silent on purpose?" Wick asked.

"That occurred to me, too." Helms paused. "It's a possibility, but there's no way of knowing for sure till we get to him."

"What does Raborn really want?"

"Meaning?"

"This all seems too flimsy. There must be something else. Something important he wants to accomplish through this arrangement. We need to know what it is," Wick said, matter-of-factly. "Josh has been an undercover operative for a long time, long enough to know some insider truths about the agency. Maybe he came across something he didn't like?"

.   .   .

Helms knew what Wick was talking about. He had been on the other side of the table and knew that the information agents were given before being sent on a mission was seldom the whole truth. Sometimes, it was quite different from ground reality. Wick knew this too, yet he went for the kill every time, without question.

"Josh is their man and yet the CIA doesn't want to get involved. Why?" Wick continued, thinking aloud.

"Maybe they don't want him back so bad," Helms offered. "Maybe it suits their purpose to have him disappear."

"If they wouldn't have wanted him back, they would have swept it under the rug and let him die. But by involving us, they've only ensured this issue will not die anytime soon," Wick said.

Helms agreed with his analysis. "What do you suggest now?" He already had a few theories on what the possible next steps could be, but he wanted to hear Wick's opinion. Wick was in the field and he knew the possibilities there. As the NSA director and the custodian of TF-77, he knew he could force agents to follow his ideas, but he didn't work like that. It was easy for him to conjure up any half-baked plan sitting in his soundproof cabin, but it was someone like Wick who would have to execute it. It was common sense to let agents take the lead on their missions.

. . .

"We should scope out the region and identify the possibilities. Do our homework before we agree to this offer. I have something in mind, but I need someone else to help me out."

"Who?"

"A sniper would be good."

"Anyone in particular?"

"Eddie."

"Eddie Vicar!" Helms suppressed his bewilderment, but Wick realized that he wasn't happy with his choice. "He's suspended."

"What happened in Lithuania wasn't completely his mistake and he still is the only one with a better trigger finger than me," Wick said. "If we are going ahead on this, I need someone like him to have my back, and he is currently in Afghanistan."

Helms thought about it. "You in touch with him?"

"Yes." Wick decided not to lie.

.   .   .

"What about his field readiness?"

"For the last six months, he is nothing but field-ready."

"Okay, talk to him."

"What will you tell Raborn?"

"I'll manage that. Also, the way he will respond to my conditions might tell us more of his intentions."

"What if he doesn't agree to wait? What if he wants to go ahead with the mission right away?" Wick asked.

"Then it's his call, it's their asset and we will steer clear," Helms said. "But Wick, I need a game plan ASAP."

"I will give you an update soon."

Satisfied, Helms disconnected the call.

CHAPTER 4

SAM WICK LOOKED at his image in the mirror, applying the finishing touches to his makeup. His eyebrows and hair were black enough not to stand out among the locals, but his blue eyes were a different story. He used color contacts to change them to dark brown. Then, he worked on turning his olive complexion duskier.

He turned around and picked the black Perahan Tunban, the preferred clothing worn by men in this part of Afghanistan, along with a jaded full-sleeve coat. The clothes were oversized and hung loosely on him, hiding his athletic frame.

He checked his possessions one last time. His upper garment had concealed compartments in which he stashed two passports and fifty grand in the local currency. One of the passports was American. It had Wick's real photograph with blue eyes and olive complexion, an alias, and stamps showing that he had entered the country through India. The second was an Afghan passport that showed him with dark brown eyes and a dusky complexion, the way he looked now. Both passports had credit cards taped to them while the Afghan passport also had a debit card. They were his way out of the country if things went haywire.

No one at the TF-77 knew about these two passports. Wick was in a profession where the tables could turn against him anytime, where it took only an instant for predator to become prey. In such a situation, it was best to hold some cards close to one's chest.

Wick had been roaming in this turbulent Asian country for the past five months and his understanding of the locales, the lingo and the accents had only deepened over time. The main roads, the railway lines, the hidden alleyways, and the shady streets, were all well-etched in his memory. Still, he carried a tiny GPS unit in his old, rugged, plain-looking Casio watch to ensure he knew where he was if he ever got into trouble.

He chose not to always carry a gun on him, but he was rarely without his trusted matte-black Ka-Bar blade concealed in the right sleeve of his coat.

In his right ear, he bore a tiny wireless communication device, hidden beneath his long sweeping hair, held in check with a traditional keffiyeh.

. . .

Once certain he had everything he would need, he opened a hidden application on his cell phone and keyed in the passcode. It was an app created by the US Department of Defense that ran as a background process on his phone. It was used by the agents in the field to receive important data and intel in regions with low or no internet connectivity. The email folder of the app showed one unread message—from his handler, Riley. The message was crisp and had an encrypted attachment—intel on Josh that Wick had asked for. Wick skimmed the rest of the email for the password.

Sending files securely over disparate servers across the globe generally needed a sophisticated high-priced security system but DoD had found a simple, but effective, method to tackle this. They'd bury the file's password key in the email's content that spelled out differently for every operative, depending on their handler's details, their coordinates, their individual key passcode and their alias for that mission. The file used a dynamic password generation technique, meaning, for two different operatives, there would be two different passwords for opening the same file. Not only that, the files would have unique mission specifics, in addition to common details, based on the recipient.

Wick synced his phone with his laptop and opened the file on the bigger screen. It was around fifty pages long, most of it redacted. Josh had obviously done a lot of work for the CIA. The first page of the report had a grainy image of Josh Fletcher at the top right. His name, vital stats and his time in the agency were listed on the left. The second page had more details on the missions he had been on, although most of the text was redacted. Wick looked through the file and then came back to the first page. He looked closely at the man he had been tasked to find. Josh Fletcher's green eyes gazed right back at him from a gaunt, bearded face.

CHAPTER 5

WICK CLOSED the back door of the safe house behind him. Five minutes later, he was walking among the handful of people on the streets of Gereshk, a sleepy town in the Helmand province of Afghanistan. The thin crowd was normal for two reasons. First, it was seven in the morning, and second, a few days ago, the Taliban had attacked one of the two hospitals in the town, killing over thirty civilians and defenseless patients. The attack had come just two days after the Afghan military had announced that its month-long "Shaheen-100" operation had killed three hundred Taliban fighters in the Nangarhar province, a Taliban stronghold. That attack, in turn, had been prompted by an earlier attack, two weeks prior, in which an improvised explosive device (IED) blast had injured three U.S. soldiers in Jalalabad, the capital city of Nangarhar. In these bloody tit-for-tat battles that played out on the streets and towns of Afghanistan, it was the civilians who were inevitably caught in the crossfire.

Wick knew the U.S. war in Afghanistan was as good as over, and that it had ended in failure. Military strikes and raids against a resurgent Taliban happened from time to time, but as soon as the U.S. forces captured or killed a few, new blood was instantly infused from neighboring countries like Pakistan. The money to fund this recruitment came predominantly from the opium trade.

Helmand was the main hub of poppy cultivation. Had it been an independent country, it would have been the largest opium producer in the world. In its current state, it contributed to about half of Afghanistan's supply, and the Taliban controlled every key poppy-growing field in Helmand. The group extracted an estimated four billion dollars from opium every year. Money that went a long way in one of the world's poorest regions. Opium profits helped the Taliban buy guns, pay salaries to its army of thirty thousand mercenaries and keep the hiring engine warm.

Despite a crackdown by the US and Afghan forces, new people joined the trade almost every day. For most rural households, the only livelihood alternative to this was to send their sons to join the Afghan security forces, which, in many cases was as good as a death sentence. Far better to have the sons cultivate poppy and pay taxes to the Taliban or the government-linked local powerbrokers. In plain words, there was simply nothing in Afghanistan that produced more jobs than the opium economy.

Wick had seen the devastating effect of the drugs on the Afghan youth. The whole country was either wielding guns or doing lines.

· · ·

Wick walked down the broken road, taking in the bombed-out skeletons of buildings, the near-deserted roads and the non-existent social life of the town. Beyond the town, there was only barren land as far as the eye could see. It was hard to keep the grief and disenchantment in check. His problem with the people who supported these wars was the extreme violence inflicted on innocent civilians, that was not only physical but also emotional and social. And despite knowing everything, he could do nothing to stop it. This was a war for an illusionary peace that Wick knew would never arrive.

He shook his head and tried to re-focus on the job at hand. His destination was a burnt-down police station just outside town. He hoped to find Akram there. The last time he had seen the man, was a month ago. Wick knew if anyone could nudge him in the right direction it was Akram. If he wasn't already dead from a drug overdose, that is. He was Wick's strongest source and without him this would be a different game altogether.

CHAPTER 6

WICK PREFERRED WALKING on Afghan roads, as Taliban fighters fired indiscriminately at running vehicles they didn't recognize as their own, and he didn't want to get shot at without reason. He maintained a steady pace, neither lingering nor hurrying, just right to not raise suspicion. That was the reason it took him forty-five minutes to reach the burned-out police station.

At the iron gate, Wick paused for a moment to gauge his surroundings. His posture was that of a local, someone indifferently looking at the carnage, but his eyes acutely examined the structure for any incongruities. The abandoned police station was a two-story construction with multiple holes for snipers. An IED blast had destroyed the building's left flank hence the frame was somewhat lopsided to the left. The right flank was still erect but could give away anytime. The walls that had been white once were now charred black, possibly from the fire that had followed the blast.

. . .

Wick looked for movement in the building. Listened for any sound. His palms were open, facing the structure. His position was of absolute vulnerability, standing at the gate, alone and unarmed. Anyone pointing a gun at him would have relished such an easy target.

After a pause of two minutes, he walked towards the building, his steps measured and quiet. A fearful posture masked his alert competence. It was imperative to be seen as harmless and frightened in the open.

At the edge of the missing wooden door of the police station, he stopped once more. He bent slightly forward to peer inside. The first thing he noticed was the smell. The building reeked of charred dead bodies. He crossed the threshold and found himself in a mid-size hall. Where once there must have been bustling activity, there was only an eerie silence left. The smell had woken up all his sensory receptors. His eyes were more alert, his demeanor had changed, and his mind worked overtime to find anything out of place.

He searched the two holding cells on the first floor. The steel bars were damaged, the small window opposite the bars was now a big hole because of what looked like a rocket blast. The wall between the two cells was blown away.

He strode towards the room to his left. The wooden plaque above the door frame said that it was a weapons store. Now only an empty shell. Someone had stolen the weapons long back, but the room could still be a good hideout. Wick made a mental note of it, then proceeded towards the stairs. There was nothing else on the first floor worth scrutiny.

What if Akram, the man he was looking for, had left the building. Even worse, what if he was in no state to talk? He would find out soon.

Wick climbed the stairs to the second floor of the building, rubble crunching under his shoes.

This floor had three rooms in relatively good condition. Once, perhaps, they had been used as temporary dwellings for the station lieutenants, but now they lay abandoned.

Wick entered the room closest to the stairs, but two steps in and he knew it was uninhabited.

The second room was locked but a man-sized hole in the wall to the right of the door frame allowed him to check that the room was vacant.

The last room of the floor was in a habitable condition. The door was missing but the stone flooring was clear of the wreckage. Inside, a shoulder-high brick divider separated the room into two.

. . .

Wick saw a foot sticking out of a cramped spot between the brick divider and the wall. There was someone in the room.

"Akram, is it you?" Wick uttered in the friendliest tone he could manage. "It's me, Omar, your friend." He quickly introduced himself with the alias Akram knew him by, speaking slowly and softly so as not to scare the man into doing anything nasty.

He didn't have to wait long for a response. "Friend?" a meek voice came from behind the barrier.

"I've brought you some stuff." Wick took out a plastic bag with brown coarse powder from the inside pocket of his coat, displaying it in the open while slowly negating the distance between him and the barrier. He had still not seen Akram's face. His eyes firmly tracing the movement of the foot, he took a curved trajectory towards the spot, maintaining his distance, and saw Akram lying on a mattress resting on a concrete block.

"Akram!" Wick whispered his name again.

The man shifted his weight on the bedding and cocked his head to look at Wick.

"Omar, is that you?"

.   .   .

"Yes, I'm here. You okay?"

"I knew you would come. I knew it." There was an unusual glee in his voice.

Wick remained where he was, watching Akram struggle to lift himself up on the mattress. After an arduous ten minutes, he was able to come to a sitting position, leaning against the wall for support. He wore a torn police uniform, and his yellowish skin was peeling off, perhaps due to an excess of drugs, or perhaps because he suffered from some skin ailment, Wick couldn't tell for sure. He made sure to not touch him or go any closer than was needed.

"Did you bring it?" Akram's voice trembled in anticipation. He was staring at the floor, purposely not making eye contact with Wick.

"Yes," Wick said.

Akram extended his right hand, palm open.

"I need something first." Wick put the plastic bag back in his pocket.

.   .   .

"How many times I have told you, I know nothing," Akram shouted. His lips curled with hate and the corner of his mouth frothed with anger. He still did not make eye contact. His tongue flicked out repeatedly, licking his lips.

"You don't know what I want," Wick said in a low whisper.

Akram said nothing.

"You know about an American reporter gone missing today?"

This time Akram raised his eyes to look at Wick. For a fleeting moment their eyes met, then Akram lowered his eyes again, staring at the floor.

"I know nothing." His body shivered.

"Okay, if you want to play it like this." Wick turned around to leave.

Akram saw his patron leaving and his mind rebelled against him. His body ached for the promised dose. His hands wanted to strangle Wick to death or crack open his skull. He could have done any of those things once, but now he was just an empty shell of his older self.

.   .   .

"Wait, please wait," Akram pleaded. He was still a salaried police officer, but without a station and with a drug problem. It was his network of informants across the Helmand province that had kept him alive so far. Wick had discovered this very early during his stay in Afghanistan. He had met him as a civilian and soon understood that Akram fed information for cash to the various armed forces acting against the Taliban. This barter system had grown to include opium too, and Akram had had a good thing going for him. But then the regime changed, and what had been Akram's selling point was now used by the new government itself to get US financial aid, making him redundant. However, he still had a few people who came to him for intel and that kept him alive. Wick was one of them.

Wick stopped and turned to face him.

"I know about the American."

"I'm listening," Wick said.

"They'll kill me if they know I snitched."

"Who will tell them? We are the only ones here." Wick took out the packet again. "But if you do not get this soon, then you will definitely be dead before the next time I see you." Akram's eyes trailed the packet.

. . .

"What do you want to know?"

"Who took him and where?"

"Why?"

"None of your concern." Wick was in no mood to oblige his curiosity.

Akram wiggled as if he were trying to unshackle his chains. "Give me some of that, I'll die if I don't get it right now."

"Enough of your games, Akram. The next thing I want to hear from you is the answer to my questions."

"I knew you would come when I heard about that American," Akram screamed, gnashing his teeth. His eyes flamed with fury. With no warning, he leaped from the bed onto Wick and dug his nails into his skin. Wick took a step back. His grasp on the bag loosened, but it still hung from his little finger. He regained his balance and hurled a blow at Akram's temple. Akram sprawled back on the mattress with a horrible groan.

Wick knelt, looking Akram straight in the eye. He spoke softly, enunciating each word. "If you ever do something like that again, I will break every bone of your body."

. . .

"I just want that bag. Please... please, I'll die."

"You won't. But if you lie, I will kill you. And you can't do shit about it."

"The Taliban took him." Akram had no other option.

"Where?"

"There is a place not far from here, near the Pakistan–Afghanistan border. I don't know the exact location, but..." Akram appeared to doze off. A sharp slap brought him around. He growled in return, trying to hit back but then curbed his instincts.

"Where?" Wick repeated.

"It's a new place," Akram mumbled, wiping his spittle.

"New place?"

"It wasn't there a few months ago. Now it's the only place where they take traitors to kill them."

.   .   .

Wick said nothing, giving Akram a long look, trying to ascertain if he was telling the truth.

"I'm not lying," Akram yelled, reading his thoughts.

"Where is it?"

"I don't know," Akram mumbled to himself but then saw Wick moving aggressively forward. "I... I... I know a man who could take you to the place."

"Who?"

"Wasim…. Wasimullah. He is a deputy commander in the Taliban. He and his team grabbed your man."

"Where would I find him?"

"You out of your mind? He has an army. If he comes to know about you, he will not just stop at you. He will kill your family, and everyone you know, just for fun."

.   .   .

"You are concerned about me. I'm touched." Wick said, sarcastically.

"What's this American to you?" Akram raised his sweaty face. His eyes were moist, and lips parched.

Wick stayed silent.

"Omar, I pity you."

"Address," Wick said, cranking up the pressure.

Akram's face contorted as he dwelled hard on his options.

"I don't have time, and neither do you." Wick dangled the bag, pressing further.

"Wasim will be in the town to meet his mother." Akram broke under pressure.

"When?"

"Today."

.   .   .

"Where?"

"I need that bag first"

Wick handed him the bag. Akram blurted out the address and withdrew eagerly into his shell with his prize. Wick looked at him snorting the powder greedily. It would probably be his final dose.

CHAPTER 7

STANDING in the shadow of the building, Wick took out a burner phone from his coat's inner pocket and dialed Eddie's number from memory.

"It's me," he said as soon as the call connected.

"Good to hear your voice."

"Need your help."

"Last time I heard, they asked me to stay out. The word they used, if I recall right, was 'loose cannon'."

"Not anymore."

· · ·

"Says who?" Eddie asked.

"Helms."

"Helms?… William Helms?"

"I don't know anyone else with that name."

"I haven't received any orders."

"These are your orders. You in or out? If you're happy to bide your time on that military base, doing paperwork while the other soldiers bore you with fake stories of their bravado, be my guest." Wick clearly wasn't interested in stretching the conversation more than it was necessary.

Eddie thought about it for a moment. "What do you want me to do?"

"You don't want to know what's in it for you?" Wick asked.

"I'm all ears." Eddie chuckled.

"Note down this address first."

.   .   .

"Okay."

Wick gave Eddie a drill down of Josh, Wasim and his upcoming visit to his mother's house. Eddie listened, asked a few questions and then was off to work.

By the time Eddie reached out to his commanding officer, the CO had already received a call from his boss about the Eddie's new assignment which he received with surprise.

What could they want from this paper pusher? That was all he could think when Eddie came to him.

His doubts were legit. Eddie, an El Paso stock with a boyish grin, black hair, and vital green eyes, was unlike the muscular officers in his unit. He was short and wiry and more importantly, a good for nothing recruit.

It was on his boss's order that he had to take Eddie in, as someone who could help the CO with the mounting paperwork, and Eddie could not be sent to the field without explicit permission from the higher-ups.

He hated Eddie from the word go. The reasons were many. One of them was that he knew nothing about the new recruit except that he was in Afghanistan for the last eight months. Secondly, he had no say in his appointment to his unit, and third, and the most important one was that he knew, Eddie was there just to bide his time, unlike others who were there for their country. And for the CO, it was the most selfish thing a soldier could do.

Being a part of the TF-77, it was a regular protocol to re-assign the assets to the nearest army units as someone who amounted to nothing. This was important as a part of their cover although, in the case of Eddie, it was, in fact, his partial suspension for not adhering to the orders.

Eddie knew all this. He also knew that the CO hated him. He knew that he didn't fit in the unit. All this amplified his problems, but this was the closest he could have been to the battlefield. So, he kept his head down and was biding his time silently, until today.

Standing in the hall of the police station, Wick gazed outside. Even under a new sun, the landscape was still devoid of men. An eerie silence filled the beautiful scenery. Wick stepped out and started to walk towards the safe house. A few minutes later, he fell into a slow jog. He had to do something else before Eddie came back to him with Wasim's whereabouts.

CHAPTER 8

A PAIR OF EYES, watched Wick through a pair of military grade binoculars from the top of a building some five hundred yards away from the police station. The man watched Wick speaking to someone on the phone and then leaving on foot, the same way he had arrived, until he became a tiny dot in the vast expanse of barren land. Once the man was sure that Wick wasn't coming back, he grabbed his bag, threw his equipment inside and ran for the stairs.

The man dressed in a white t-shirt, khaki pants, and clubman sunglasses hopped into his Toyota SUV parked behind the building, hidden beneath a green cover.

He turned the ignition on and raced to the Police Station. Instead of parking near the front gate, he drove the SUV to the back of the building. The tire marks already present on the sand testified to the SUV's previous visit in the not-so-distant past.

. . .

In the room on the second floor, Akram was on the verge of dozing off when someone grabbed him by his collar and yanked him out of his makeshift shelter.

Akram was in no condition to fight back. The man slapped him hard and flung to the floor like he was a ragdoll. The back of Akram's head hit the concrete and he cried out in pain.

"Are you out of your mind?" Akram yelled.

"Good that you are in your senses. What have you told him?"

"Whatever you asked me to. Where is my money?" Akram grunted.

The man ignored his question, walking towards the only window of the room.

"Where's my money?" Akram's voice trailed him.

The man peered outside the window. A tiny grey recorder was stuck in the space between two bricks. He carefully plucked it out. He then took out a listening device from his pocket and plugged it into the recorder. For the next few minutes, he listened to the recording, occasionally rewinding and forwarding the recording. Once he was sure he had captured every nuance of their conversation, he turned his attention back to Akram, who was staring at him incredulously.

"When did you…" Akram faltered when he saw the man taking out a silenced gun. "No… No…" Akram tried to crawl away but the first two bullets unerringly found their way into his skull.

CHAPTER 9

EDDIE GOT off the hired three-wheeler, three blocks away from the location. He intended to walk the rest of the distance. In a busy neighborhood, mixing in with the locals was vital. Eddie looked like a professor wearing a blue perahan tunban with black-rimmed round glasses. On his right shoulder he carried a duffle bag that matched perfectly with his overall outfit and carried everything he needed.

The most important thing in the bag was a pair of Steiner military binoculars. With an astonishing 6500-yard range, the binoculars were high on precision. With an 8X magnification and a weight of 33 oz, it was useful for missions like these and perfect for someone like him who preferred to travel light.

It didn't take him long to find the target location. It was the only house with two guards at the front door, brandishing loaded assault rifles. Eddie ambled past the house without making eye contact with either of the two gunmen. He walked to the end of the road and took a right. Once he crossed the bend, he increased his pace, covering the next two blocks quickly. Halfway through the third block, he found a six-story under-construction building with a perfect vantage point of the house.

He skimmed the neighborhood for any onlookers, anyone who could pose a problem. The locality was deserted. The time was eleven in the morning and people were probably off to work. Without losing an extra second, he walked into the building. He found the stairs to his right. Taking multiple strides at a time, he reached the top of the building in no time. On the rooftop, he took out the binoculars and immediately pinned down the house. At 6X magnification, he could clearly see the front porch secured by the two men he had walked past. He took out a tiny earpiece with a mic and stuck it in his ear.

"Eddie checking in."

On the other side, Wick's earpiece crackled.

"What's the situation?"

"Stationed on the sixth floor of an under-construction building, three blocks south of the target. Two tangos securing the front door. No other movement. The target possibly has not yet arrived."

.   .   .

"Okay, stay put. I'll be there soon."

Eddie didn't have to wait long. Some thirty minutes later, three open Toyota SUVs turned into the street. One by one they came to a gentle halt in front of the house. Doors of the first and the third SUV opened. Four men with Kalashnikov assault rifles emerged from each vehicle. On any other street in the world, this would have caused immediate panic, but this was Afghanistan. There was barely a ripple. Once they secured the perimeter, the second SUV opened, and a man got out. Wasim, Eddie guessed, though he had no way of knowing for sure.

Eddie tapped for Wick on the earpiece but found only static. He was off the grid. Eddie was three blocks away and if the cavalcade moved again, he had no way to tail it.

He decided to keep his focus on the one-story house and wait for Wick.

CHAPTER 10

THE MEN from the SUVs disappeared into the house, and the street became like any other.

Close to the house, a group of eight- to ten-year-old boys was playing cricket.

The batsman was a lanky boy, just under four feet in height, while the kid at the bowler's end was thin and short, looking a year younger than the batsman. His face turned red as he took a long run-up for pitching the ball at the batsman. His sprint was fast and steady. He released the ball from the top of his hand with a nice inward angle. The ball hit the uneven pitch and remained low. The batsman was ready; he expertly maneuvered the uneven bounce and swung his bat. There was a loud thwack of the ball hitting wood, and the ball soared skywards. A boy fielding at the boundary misjudged the trajectory and started his sprint a second too late. The ball came down, bounced across the street and rolled under the third SUV. The fielder came running and peered under the SUV. The ball wasn't there. He walked around the SUV and knelt on the ground looking all around. No sign of the ball still.

"Did you see any ball here?" the boy asked one of the two gunmen securing the house.

"This is not a playground," one of them snapped.

"Where is it?" The boy looked around, not listening.

"Go away." The gunman made a shooing gesture, but the kid was unyielding. The man finally gave up and lifted his right boot. The ball rolled forward. The boy saw it. These men were toying with him and he didn't like it one bit. The ball rolled slowly and stopped in front of the man, but the kid remained in his place, waiting for their move. His stance indicated that he did not want to take the ball from the man's feet.

The man was in no mood to oblige the kid. He raised his right leg and swung it forward, kicking the ball away from the boy. The ball spun in the air and hit the second SUV, bounced once, spun away from the child, hit the SUV again and then rolled beneath the vehicle.

"That's your ball. Now get lost."

. . .

The boy gave the men an angry glare. He bent again on his knees and extended his left hand to grab the ball but despite his best efforts, the ball remained elusive. He then lay on his stomach and rolled beneath the SUV, smearing his clothes. This time the ball couldn't escape his grasp. He rolled back out. Soon he was on his feet again, staring back at the guards. Then, he was off, laughing.

The unexpected laugh surprised the gunmen, but they had no way of knowing what was going on in the mind of that little devil. They went back to their conversation, the boy forgotten. Eddie had been watching the whole scene unfold before his binocular-enhanced eyes. Finding the boy's behavior strange, he kept the binoculars trained on the kid.

Instead of returning to the game, the boy went to a shop near the house. Eddie augmented the magnification to 8X. The kid walked up to a man in the shop. The man extended his hand and gave the boy what looked like a currency note. Eddie shifted focus to the man's face and a smile came on his face. It was Wick behind heavy makeup.

The game was on.

CHAPTER 11

"WICK, IS THAT YOU?" Eddie whispered in the earpiece to confirm.

"Yes," Wick whispered.

"Was that Wasim?"

"Yes."

"Okay."

"Any movement?" Wick's vision was hindered by the stationary SUVs, he knew Eddie had a better vantage point.

· · ·

Eddie saw the guards straightening up. "Yes. the door has opened."

The man they knew to be Wasim came out. Eddie checked his watch. He had spent exactly forty minutes in the house. One of the two guards hurried forward and held the door of the second SUV open for him. The driver was already alert behind the wheel, and the minute Wasim settled into the passenger seat, the three vehicles sped away.

Eddie saw the convoy moving. He then looked at Wick whose eyes were following the SUVs down the road.

"Eddie." His earpiece crackled with Wick's voice. "I have sent you the coordinates. Meet me there."

Eddie threw the binoculars in the bag, zipped it up and sprinted towards the stairs. The location was a mere five-minute run from the building. An old Ford was waiting for him, its engine running. Wick was behind the wheel, Eddie opened the door and settled down in the seat beside him. The Ford rolled forward. There was a military grade GPS device on the dashboard with a moving red dot. Eddie recognized the device— it was a standard DoD product. The location on the screen was accurate up to eight meters with a 0.01% lag time—the closest thing one could get to real-time location tracking.

"The red dot is Wasim?"

.   .   .

Wick nodded in affirmative.

Eddie grinned in understanding. "How much did you pay the boy?"

"A couple of hundreds. Anyway, there is something for you in the back."

Eddie turned in his seat and found his own duffle bag on the passenger seat. He grabbed its handle, pulled it closer and opened the zipper.

"You brought my sweetie. When did you get the time?"

"One of my contacts stationed at your Army base delivered it to me. Everything's there?"

Inside was a .300 Win-Mag—a bolt-action sniper rifle. Unlike other snipers, Eddie preferred this beauty because of its superiority over others. Being a heavier weapon by design, it drilled its deadly payload into its targets like a laser. With this in hand, anything from a thousand yards and out was toast. Even on closer targets, Eddie didn't have to worry too much about correction for the come-ups.

.   .   .

The red dot moved at a steady speed and was soon out of the city. Wick glanced at the map—one of the likely destinations was Panjwai, a district in the Kandahar province, also the spiritual home of the Taliban. Their fears turned to reality very soon as the dot moved towards the Panjwai and then took a turn towards Zangabad, a village in the Panjwai district and one of the four villages considered the birthplace of the Taliban.

Wick stopped the vehicle and stared at Eddie. They both knew Zangabad's history. It was the burial site of hundreds of NATO soldiers, murdered at the hands of the Taliban. If Josh Fletcher was in Zangabad, then there was almost no chance of his survival.

CHAPTER 12

OVAL OFFICE, **Washington**

President Greg Hancock had been in office for almost twenty months and, in those months, he had rewritten history books by being one of the most unpopular presidents in the modern era. His latest weekly approval ratings languished at thirty-five percent, far below that of any of his predecessors. That wasn't too surprising, given the fact that when he had assumed office twenty months ago, he had had the lowest approval rating of any incoming president, having won the election with anemic numbers.

Before being elected President, Hancock had been the CEO of a casino enterprise. The man from Cincinnati had been elected to the highest office in the land largely because of his divisive policies and his hardline approach towards immigrants whom he proclaimed a threat to America. He had berated previous administrations for being soft on immigration, and that was the main reason he now sat in the Oval Office.

Personally too, Hancock was going through a rough phase. His third wife, an ex-Playboy model, had decided not to appear in public with him, thanks to the allegations of his affairs with his campaign secretary. His three children from his previous marriages had already disowned him. All in all, Hancock was very lonely at the top.

Now with the US midterm elections approaching, he was under extreme pressure to deliver on his campaign promises of making the country safer and getting better returns on the aid the U.S. gave various countries. Worse, he suspected that parts of his administration were actively working against him; God knew there were enough people in D.C. and beyond who would love to see him crash and burn. Topping his list of potential adversaries was William Helms.

Hancock saw the NSA director as a threat. The overt reason was the latter's neutral response to Hancock's political ideology which Helms' considered as being against American values. The other, and more disturbing, reason that only a few people knew —and Helms was not one of those people—was that the President suspected him of putting together a file on him through a covert ops team, TF-77. The contents of that file, Hancock worried, could be used to indict and impeach him. The problem was that Hancock had no access to the team or what it does because of the way it was created by his predecessor in the first place. The rationale behind this had been that the team was involved in things that could lead to congressional hearings and even indictment if the President was found to be aware of its mission specifics.

Hancock thought it was bullshit. Maybe his predecessor wasn't very certain of his own political acumen, which was why he had needed this veil, but Hancock was no moron. If he could be the President of the world's strongest economy, then he was smart enough to know how the missions that no other team could do were executed by TF-77. But unfortunately, it was Helms who always acted as a shield against his attempts to gain control of TF-77 by using legal terms. That uneasy equation between them was the reason why Hancock's paranoia of being backstabbed was noticeable in his dealings with the NSA director, but he had so far found no evidence of Helms having gone against him. Maybe Helms was waiting for the right moment, and Hancock had sleepless nights trying to guess what that would be.

Now, as he sat at his desk in the Oval Office, waiting to be patched into a video conference with Helms, his mind raced with various calculations.

Helms was surprised when he got a call from the White House just an hour after his chat with Raborn.

President Greg Hancock had a decent working relationship with both the Pentagon and the CIA, but with NSA it was a different story altogether. Helms was aware of that.

.   .   .

Helms, despite his opinions on White House policies, had invariably adhered to the professional courtesy expected of him while dealing with the Oval Office. He had no dreams of a political career or a future place in the White House. He was happy being in Maryland as long as they allowed him to be there, and that made him state his opinions fearlessly every single time.

It took Helms an hour to reach his office after the call from the White House. He checked his watch. The video conference was due in fifteen minutes. Helms sighed. His day off was turning out to be very different from what he had planned.

The screen lit up right on time. Hancock was in his high-backed leather chair, talking to someone on the phone. The walls of the room were paneled with dark wood except for a white square section behind the president's chair. In the middle of that section was the familiar circular seal of the President of the United States. And that's when Helms saw Raborn in the room with the president. His sense of unease soared, and he knew in that instant that he had walked into a trap.

"Good afternoon Mr. President," Helms said, maintaining his composure.

"Afternoon, Bill." President Hancock placed a hand over the mouthpiece and said, "I'll be with you in a minute."

. . .

Helms said nothing. He did not understand what the agenda of this impromptu meeting was, but he knew the suspense wouldn't last long.

"It has come to my attention that one of the CIA assets in Afghanistan is missing. I want the Task Force-77 to take a lead on this," Hancock came right to the point as soon as his call was over.

"Mr. President, with due respect, I already had a chat with the CIA director on this and we are still mulling over our options on how best to approach this situation. Without a go-ahead from my men in the field, I cannot authorize this mission."

"You cannot authorize this mission?" Hancock's condescending tone boomed through the speakers. "No one here has asked for your permission to authorize this. As far as I know, TF-77 was created to take up missions exactly like this one so that our crit- ical assets can be shielded. Based on the intel, this is a mission tailor-made for that team. I just want them to do what they signed up for. And Helms, let's not forget I am not only your boss but also the President of this country, and I want the best people on this job." He paused to watch Helms's reaction. He had hoped to see the man squirming but all he saw was a steely determination. He decided to continue. "I'm green-lighting this mission and I don't want to hear any bullshit about policies and procedures. Get it done."

.   .   .

"Mr. President, with all due respect, I am not bullshitting anyone here." Helms was standing now, with both hands on his desk and his eyes piercing the screen. He had to protect his assets, Wick and Eddie. "Without significant information about the situation, I cannot commit to an action that may have further negative repercussions. The CIA also has agents placed in the region and if Raborn is so keen to go ahead with the mission, he already has enough resources at his disposal."

"Raborn has already briefed me on what his agents can and cannot do. These men are deeply entrenched in the Taliban network and, thanks to the information shared by them, many of the current U.S. operations against the outfit have been so successful. We are not going to compromise their positions because you don't want to send your men in there. And what has the NSA or this task force of yours done to secure our borders or our men on the battlefield since I have taken charge of this office? Are you suggesting we should blow the covers of our invaluable assets because you care more about red tape over the life of a man? Is that just because he is not from your agency?" Hancock got to his feet too, mimicking Helms posture, his eyes fixated on Helms.

The accusations aroused a deep rage in Helms. Everyone in the room knew they were nothing but the result of a scheming mind.

"Bill, I want this man free within the next twelve hours. Tomorrow morning, I am tabling an amendment to pull American forces out of Afghanistan. We cannot afford this man's death and you cannot afford to get on the wrong side of the President of the

United States. Make sure this man lives. If you cannot, or will not, then I want your resignation on my desk in the next ten minutes. Do you understand me?" Hancock thundered. Behind him, Raborn gave a sly grin.

"Mr. President, if we carry out these orders, chances are that we not only will lose the CIA agent, but also our other assets on the ground. Won't it hamper the amendment then?" Helms kept his face calm, keeping a lid on his anger.

"Let me take care of the politics of that. Your job is to carry out my orders." Hancock stood and pulled on his cufflinks. "I will be at the Kennedy Center. Keep me updated." With that, he disconnected the live feed.

CHAPTER 13

WICK TOOK a sharp turn to his right, driving the Ford away from the red dot. In regular circumstances, he would have planned his moves on the go, but this was different. He needed to have some sort of blueprint before he could take the next step.

Eddie looked at him and shared his dilemma. The same thoughts were in his head. Despite his stellar record as a sniper, he had never been in this section of the country largely due to NATO's reluctance. They had lost enough people to have a go at it again.

Wick drove the Ford for a couple of miles in the intense heat before he found a safe place to park and apprise Helms about the situation. He picked his satellite phone and dialed the number from memory. Helms picked up on the second ring.

"Yes, Wick."

. . .

"They are possibly holding the target at Zangabad," Wick said and paused. He wanted Helms to grasp the gravity of the situation before giving his take on things. Helms knew what Zangabad meant. This mission was doomed from the start and that was why Raborn had gone behind his back to get the President on his side.

"What do you suggest now?" he asked.

"Two options. One, after assessing the situation and knowing the terrain, Eddie and I go in and try to extract Josh. The probability of success is less than one percent. Two, we do not go ahead with the mission, and instead ask the CIA to engage with the Taliban and we'll back them up."

Helms heard him out without interrupting. He knew he had to deliver the bad news now. "Two is not an option anymore." He spoke firmly.

"Not an option!" This time it was Eddie.

"Raborn has gone behind my back and convinced the President that the TF-77 needs to lead this mission on its own. We either do this now, or I will have to resign from both TF-77 and NSA to pave the way for someone who would not hesitate to give the go-ahead. I have already decided to resign, so if you do not intend to go ahead with the mission, I'll respect your choice."

There was a long silence on the line. It was a betrayal of the highest order that no one had seen coming, but the it was Wick and Eddie who would bear the brunt of it.

Eddie spoke first, "But it was never our headache in the first place. The CIA came to us for help."

Helms couldn't see Eddie but could sense his anger and disappointment. He said nothing.

"This is a bunch of bull!" Eddie continued. "How the hell did he convince Hancock? Why couldn't you do something about it?" The accusation was directed at Helms. Raborn and Hancock were not in charge of TF-77, Helms was. The buck stopped at him.

All this while, Wick's silence was conspicuous. He was mentally calculating the various options they had, now that the die had been cast. His mind swirled with possibilities and reasons why Raborn would do something like this.

"The President is planning to table an amendment to pull American forces out of Afghanistan. For that to happen, Josh Fletcher needs to come out of that hell alive. His death means there will be no amendment of any sort because people won't forgive the death of an American hostage on foreign soil. The pullout plan will be a bust, so he wants us to keep his plan on track," Helms explained.

. . .

"I knew he's an idiot, that's why I never voted for him. Bloody motherfucker." Eddie was livid. "And he cares about one life over two lives here. What if we die in there? Will the CIA then go and save Josh? What does he has to say about that?"

Helms had no answer to that. He had asked the same question to Hancock and got nothing much in return.

It was a valid point. If, instead of one life, America lost three, it would be all the more difficult to recall US troops out of Afghanistan. How was Hancock planning to handle such a situation?

"What's his take if we die in there?" Wick asked finally.

For a minute no one spoke. Wick and Eddie stared at the speaker with anticipation. Helms knew there was no getting out of this. He had to answer his men. He cleared his throat and then gave them the verbatim transcript of the response he had got from Hancock about his politics comment.

Listening to this Eddie was too stunned to respond. Their government didn't give a rat's ass about their existence. Dying for the nation was just a bloody farce. They were sent to the field to die. If they came back alive, it was their luck and if they failed, no one would bother.

. . .

Wick could understand why Josh's life had more value than Eddie's and his own. Josh's cover was of a CNN reporter. During the last five years, they had plastered his name on multiple articles and news reports on the CNN website even though the stories were fabricated by some lonely ghostwriter sitting in Langley. He could not disappear without questions being raised. Eddie and Wick came with no such baggage. They were just names within the corridors of the TF-77, unknown to anyone outside its glass facade. Technically, there was no Wick or Eddie for the American people. There would be no outrage even if they both went missing in this barren land. He wasn't sure even Helms would bother much. This was the harsh reality of their lives and Wick, despite being the utmost realist, at that moment felt a strong sense of betrayal by his own country.

Wick hated politicians. Men like him lived by a warrior's code— honor and integrity above everything. Do what you say and mean what you do. Politicians just said whatever would keep them in power. They were cockroaches. Washington was run by cockroaches. They had had operations exposed because those cockroaches didn't know how to keep their mouths shut. Wick had worked for months planning missions and then had the plug pulled on him at the last minute because some politician had contracted the foot-in-the-mouth disease and leaked everything to the media. They had given everything they had to their country, and in return they saw those whores in Washington selling America down the drain. Good, honest politicians were a rare, almost extinct, breed, most were lying egomaniacs who thought everything was a game.

. . .

Bloody cockroaches.

And these cockroaches had decided Wick and Eddie's life had no value. They were expendables, so they could go and raid a Taliban stronghold even NATO wouldn't dare approach. Wick seriously considered walking away from the whole mess and never looking back. Maybe it was time to use those passports.

"I know how this looks," Helms' voice came over the tiny speaker, cutting into his thoughts. "I won't blame you for not trusting me., You have every right to feel betrayed and angry. Frankly, I have the same feelings right now." This was the first time in his career that he knew he had been played and, because of his oversight, his men were being forced to under-take this suicidal mission. All because he had failed to perceive the rotten design of this deceit in time. The fact that he himself was also a part of this very system made him equally responsi-ble. "Wick… Eddie… I know…"

"Helms," Wick interrupted Helms for the first time in his life, "Just to make it clear where we stand on this, there are a lot of things that are not told to you. Stuff that you're better off not knowing, but maybe now's a good time to give you a glimpse of what it takes to get a job done." Wick was beyond caring that Helms was his boss. "During my last mission just eight days ago, the basement where our target was kept—a target TF-77 wanted dearly—that basement was underneath a house inhab-ited by a family. A family with a five-year-old boy and a pregnant woman. Obviously, McAvoy conveniently forgot to tell me that since he didn't want me to get distracted or lose sight of the mission. And when I dropped grenades inside that house, guess who died? I executed that family and even when I feel my heart rotting with guilt or my brain exploding with nightmares, I take it all without complaint. Why? Because that's what it takes to work for your country. So, don't lecture me about what or what not could have happened in that meeting, because I doubt anyone else in the government would have pulled that pin." Without waiting for his response, Wick disconnected the line.

Both Eddie and Wick sat quietly in the Ford, observing the vast horizon through the windshield. No trees as far as the eye could see. A sandstorm was brewing at a distance. They had shut Helms off, but their minds were still running the course of the different directions this job could take. Almost all of them ended with them getting a bullet in the guts for their efforts.

"What do you think?" Wick said, finally.

"Truth?"

Wick nodded. He had already made up his mind, but he wanted to know Eddie's point of view.

"We are fucked by our own government. Who would believe that? My mind tells me to back off. Fuck the orders. I don't care about Helms or Raborn or that son of a bitch Hancock."

.   .   .

"But?" Wick knew this was not it.

"But there is an agent who is going to die today if we don't act."

Wick nodded.

"I agree they have played us and Helms but still..." Eddie said.

"So, what now?" Sam said,

"Well...damned if we do, and damned if we don't," Eddie spoke without inhibition. "But, no one has ever done it and the fact that this is Taliban's home base, we could probably find them napping. I think we can pull this off. What do you think?"

"It's a big gamble."

"We owe it to Josh," Eddie said.

Wick nodded. He agreed with Eddie that if nothing else, they should do it to save an American life. To hell with the cockroaches.

· · ·

"And if we pull this one off, we will be legends," Eddie said with a grin, trying as usual to put a positive spin on their grim situation.

Wick smiled at the juvenile effort. He turned and pulled out a backpack from under the backseat. He unzipped it and took out a Panasonic Toughbook—a military-grade laptop built to withstand extreme weather conditions and terrain. The machine had always worked for him whenever he needed it. He flipped it open and it lit up like a white neon board. He then took out a USB flash drive from the bag and plugged it into the laptop. The drive had been developed by the US Department of Defense to provide internet access from the most remote locations. The only downside—the security of the drive was patchy depending on the location's internet protocols.

Wick remembered reading about an agricultural fair being inaugurated recently by the Afghan cultural minister at Panjwai. It was a part of a government initiative to promote the best agricultural practices by setting up temporary marketplaces across the villages of a district. Wick checked the dates, and then as he scrolled down the list of the villages, his lips curled into a smile. Zangabad was on the list. He shifted his gaze to the GPS. The red dot was now to the other side of the village, close to the location where the temporary market was located.

After considering all the possibilities, Wick raised his eyes from the Toughbook's screen. Eddie was watching him with a mixed expression. Wick had not spoken for the last ten minutes, and he wanted to know if there was a plan or if Wick needed more time.

·   ·   ·

"There is a way."

Eddie grinned and banged his fist on the dashboard. "I knew it. I bloody knew it. Rise and shine, baby. Rise and shine."

Wick grabbed his sat phone and dialed Helms' number. He ignored the livid expression on Eddie's face. "You're not gonna tell him the plan, are you?" Eddie asked. Wick chose not to respond.

"Sam here."

"Yes, Sam."

"We are going ahead with the job," Wick said.

Helms didn't know what to say. He could only imagine what kind of fortitude it must have taken for these two men to agree to this botched assignment. He was both worried and grateful.

"We'll talk soon." Wick revealed no details about his plan. He respected Helms but the wall of trust had been breached. Eddie might have believed Helms' innocence, but Wick needed some time, maybe forever, to rebuild that trust between him and Helms.

. . .

"All the best." Helms knew he didn't have any more than these three inadequate words to offer the men.

CHAPTER 14

THEY GOT out of the vehicle. Eddie grabbed his .300-Win mag and begin to examine it. Wick went over to the back and opened the boot.

The floor mat was clean. He raised it, making sure not to disturb what was underneath. The space beneath the mat was crammed with gear. There was a big makeup box resting at the center. A sealed pack was on its left. A fiber bag was lying to its right with a new set of clothes. Wick opened the makeup box first and checked his face in the mirror. His lenses were in place, his skin was of the right texture and his beard was of the right shade. Satisfied, he retrieved the untouched sealed pack. It had two Berettas and seven rounds of ammo. He had already dismantled them once at the safe house to check for any jammed or malfunctioning parts, but he wanted to do another check before going further. One by one, he examined the magazine release-catch mechanism, the dual recoil spring and everything else. Satisfied, he picked the one that felt more at home in his hand. He pushed a magazine in it and put three extra rounds in the specially crafted inner pockets of his coat. He then lifted the makeup box. Beneath it, there was another packet with fifty grand in local currency and another of his preferred Ka-Bar military blades. He took out the second blade and added into his armory. He then added the money from his pocket to the fifty grand in the trunk. All the while, he kept an eye on the red dot, still stationed at the same site. He put the mat back in place, reopened his laptop and keyed in the coordinates of Wasim's SUV.

"Eddie, here is the plan. This is a small rocky plateau." Wick showed Eddie a zigzag line on the map. "Do you think you can shoot from the top of this hill to this location?" He clicked a button and a straight line became visible from the hill to the location of Wasim's SUV.

Eddie saw the number next to the dotted line—more than a thousand yards. Somewhere between fourteen and fifteen hundred yards. Even with a Win Mag, this was tough. He had never taken a shot at this distance. He gazed at Wick's expression of grim grit. He seemed to have already thought through it.

"This is the only hill with a clear view of this location and the only hill outside the purview of Taliban-ruled areas. This is our only shot, can you take it?" Wick used his index finger to point out the location. The distance was just about half a mile from the SUV. "I'll find a way to be near this place in the next hour and collect more intel on the perimeter and the location."

. . .

What Wick was proposing sounded like a viable plan, but Eddie's own inadequacies made him stay silent. He was running several scenarios which invariably started with him not hitting the mark with his first shot and ending with leaving Wick on his own out in the open. The painful silence stretched for a few minutes before Eddie opened his closed arms and nodded his head. He was ready to take the plunge. Wick smiled looking at his posture. Eddie had bested his demons. The only thing left now was to take the shots when the time was right.

Wick closed his laptop after giving him the coordinates of the hill, which Eddie keyed into his GPS device. Wick then handed him the keys, and they both shook hands.

"See you soon, buddy," Eddie said.

Wick gave him a smile and headed towards Zangabad on foot.

Eddie fired the Ford's engine. The estimated time duration to his destination was forty minutes.

CHAPTER 15

A CARAVAN WAS PROCEEDING on a nonexistent road across the barren plains, carrying the tents, agricultural supplies and household items of thirty-eight traders, farmers, potters, shepherds, and their families. The majority in the group were farmers, heading towards the agricultural fair. Vast expanses of land that once were lush with crops of wheat, rice, and numerous vegetables, now lay sterile around the caravan.

The motive to undertake this long and arduous journey was a cash incentive announced by the Afghan government. They had heard good things about the fair and hoped to make some money selling their produce too, apart from the incentive. Their own village, Khewa, had just a small market on a single dirt road, lined with small wooden stalls. It had the most basic goods available at a fruit stand, a butcher shop with fly-covered meat hanging on hooks in the open, a shop selling everything from batteries to biscuits, and an abandoned music kiosk that had once stocked Persian, Pashto, and Hindi audio cassettes.

. . .

Zahoor, a young man in the group, was eager to reach Zangabad primarily to see friends he had met on his past trips through the area. This trip may not have a lot to offer, but for a twenty-year-old in Afghanistan, it was an oasis in the desert of his life.

The caravan had been on the road for the last two weeks, moving at a glacial speed of about ten miles a day. But finally, their destination was only a few minutes away.

Wick saw the hen first. Confused and scared from being away from its nest, it was cackling, occasionally pecking at the rough ground for anything worth eating. Wick drew the Ka-Bar from his inner pocket. His left eye closed with concentration. The bird glanced at him, paying him scant attention before going back to pecking the ground. Wick swung his hand, and the knife left his fingers with a whoosh. The air displacement forewarned the bird, and it darted away. Wick had anticipated its flight and accounted for it in his throw, but the bird took an unlikely direction. Still, the knife nicked its leg before burying itself in the dirt. Wick rushed forward. The fumbling, limping bird went a few steps, then collapsed. Wick picked up his knife to put it out of its misery. This time he didn't miss.

He tore the stomach lining of the dead bird. Blood drenched his palms and spattered his clothes. His disguise was now complete. He looked around and saw the caravan of camels still ambling slowly in the direction of Zangabad, a mile away. He checked his gear one last time and started to run.

CHAPTER 16

THREE PAIRS of eyes watched the prisoner through the two-way mirror in silence, evaluating his expressions, measuring his determination. They all had the same question in mind—how far would they have to go to break him?

Josh Fletcher was alone in the dank room. Sitting on an absurdly uncomfortable chair and handcuffed behind his back. Wearing only a pair of shoes, with even the laces taken away. No clothes on his body. There was no way he was going to live, he knew that. If not the Taliban, then his own men would kill him. He didn't delude himself with any notion that he was a hero. No, he was just a survivor whose time had come. The mirror on the wall facing him was two-way. He'd been in enough interrogations to know that, but he'd always been on the other side of the mirror. Till now.

The room was soundproofed to the tee, denying him even the relatable sound of human whispers from the outside. His stomach was growling, but other than that he didn't make any sound. It was futile, and he knew that. No use wasting his already depleted energy. A light bulb secured with two wires dangled a couple of feet above his head. The severe glare of the fluorescent light and his own weariness made his head sag forward, his chin resting on his chest. He was perilously close to losing his balance and tumbling over, which was precisely what his abductors craved.

WasimUllah arrived at the facility in his SUV. The other two SUVs were already gone. There was a consignment approaching the border and his orders were to secure it, but Wasim also had to check on the prisoner. He couldn't be at two places at once, so the only option was to send his men. When he entered the room, the three men scattered to give him space. Standing close to the two-way mirror, he examined the American, abducted on the orders of his commander, Abdul Basit.

Basit said the man was a CIA spy and there was no reason for Wasim to distrust that information. His faith in Basit was absolute and unflinching.

Not long ago, Wasim used to earn his living driving a rickety truck, but then he had got fired from his company for abusing his supervisor. The next day he went to the supervisor's cabin and exacted his revenge. The beating was severe, and Wasim was arrested. In prison, he met someone who knew Basit. At the time, Basit was a small-time arms supplier, actively looking for someone who wasn't averse to the associated risk of his business. Wasim took up on his offer as there wasn't any job waiting for him outside and his need for cash was snowballing every day. Basit took him under his wing— paid for his bail, gave him work and money. Soon he was an important man. Basit bought Wasim's loyalty, and now when he asked him to abduct a man he didn't know, Wasim didn't ask why.

The weather outside was bad enough, but here in the underground cemented facility, it was hell. There wasn't any air-conditioning or even an air vent. The area was lit by kerosene lanterns laboring hard against the darkness and yet losing the battle. Wasim was perspiring profusely. Sweat had already left widening dark patches on his clothes at his underarms and the neckline. The American wasn't going to last much longer in these trying conditions.

He knew Josh would talk. They all talked, eventually. No man, no matter how strong he was on the battlefield or in his training, could endure this kind of torture forever. Getting them to talk wasn't the problem. True skill lay in getting them to tell the truth. Josh was no different. So far, he had stuck to his story of being a CNN reporter in Afghanistan, a story that Wasim knew was an out-and-out lie, but he had not been grilled enough yet. He would be soon.

CHAPTER 17

ZAHOOR NOTICED the man before anyone else. The man running towards them as though his very life were at stake, waving his hands and calling out desperately, looking back every now and then like he was being hunted, his blood-soaked clothes, hands and face telling a compelling tale of survival even from afar. The other men in the caravan turned to look at him.

The scene was a shock for everyone else but for Zahoor, it was more than that. He had seen this before, with his own father. A wave of anger and fear rose in his chest.

Wick's right foot hit an insignificant rock and his speed unraveled rapidly. He swerved in the air and landed flat on the uneven ground, but that didn't stop him. His hands lifted him off the ground and his legs kicked the sand, propelling his body forward. His crawling soon turned into a struggle. Zahoor saw the man in trouble and his natural instinct was to step forward and help, but one of the boys grabbed his arm reminding him of his place.

Wick noticed Zahoor's keenness and identified the benefactor who could help him get into the group without much resistance. He struggled to his feet and altered his course.

By the time he reached the caravan, he was panting hard, his heartbeat was through the roof, his eyes were watery, and his throat parched. He bent over, hands on knees, wheezing.

Zahoor could not resist this time. He stepped forward to help Wick but before he could grab him by the shoulder, Wick clutched Zahoor's left hand. His eyes met with Zahoor's who saw a pair of fearful brown eyes on a bloodied weather-beaten face. He signaled the nearest person to get some water. The boy, despite his reluctance, didn't have the heart to refuse the visibly shattered man. He ran and got a small bottle of water. Zahoor handed it to Wick who took it gratefully and gulped it down in one breath, his eyes closed.

Wick splashed the last few drops on his face, getting rid of the blood from his eyelids.

"Thank you." Wick's eyes were moist with gratitude.

"Who are you?"

. . .

"I'm Omar from Mushan village. I went to Kandahar market, with my father, to sell our goats. On our way home, some local dacoits attacked us. We fought hard, but they had numbers on their side. They killed my father, but I managed to escape." Wick's sobs grew heavier as his story reached its sad ending. He could see Zahoor and the elders of the caravan shaking their heads in sympathy.   "I just need to get to Zangabad, my maternal uncle lives there. Can you please take me with you to the village? It's very near, but I'm scared they will find me again. Please, please help me." Wick was on his knees, pleading with his hands folded. It was a gut-wrenching sight for everyone, a man pleading for his life.

The elders of the group glanced at each other. Wick watched them go into a huddle away from everyone, his eyes full of hope, his face wet with tears. The success of his plan rested on those select few.

"What do you say?" the first elder asked an open question.

"We don't know him. How can we trust him?" the man standing next to him protested.

"But we cannot leave him in this condition," a third man chipped in.

. . .

"What if his assailants attack us also?" the fourth chimed in.

"Then we cannot stay here for long. Zangabad is only thirty minutes from here.

We need to keep moving," the first man said in a worried tone, scanning the horizon.

"We still need to decide about him," the fourth one said, looking at Wick from the corner of his eyes.

"If he is saying that his uncle will meet him in Zangabad then we only need to take him till there and then he's on his own," the third man reasoned.

"His blood-soaked clothes can be a problem for us when we enter the village. There will be questions."

"I have clean spare clothes he could wear. We can hide him," Zahoor said quickly, seeing an opportunity to sway the decision.

The four elders looked at each other. There was no unanimous decision on Wick. They were worried about the dacoits, but a desperate man was in need and Allah wouldn't be kind to them if they left him to die. Finally, one of the elders glanced at Zahoor and nodded. It was all he needed. Wick saw Zahoor's lips widening into a smile, and he knew they had agreed to take him with them.

"You need to change into these." Zahoor handed a set of spare clothes to Wick with an encouraging smile. "Your clothes are no longer usable. You can put them in this." He handed him a cotton bag.

Wick hadn't seen this coming. He knew he could not give up his coat. It had everything he needed.

"This coat is the last thing from my father before his death. Please don't take it from me, I will wear the rest as you wish," Wick pleaded with moist eyes.

Zahoor stared at Wick. His own situation had been similar once. He smiled and agreed but decided not to discuss this with the elders. He knew they wouldn't be thrilled about it.

Wick got behind a sitting camel, away from everyone's eyes and changed swiftly into the new clothes. He soon donned a long kurta and pajama. They ill-fitted him but his movement wasn't hampered. That's all he needed.

The caravan started its journey again with Wick walking along with the others. Thirty-five minutes later, they were at the village entrance.

CHAPTER 18

THE FORD CAME to a halt near the foot of the rocky hill. Killing the engine, Eddie started his labored climb on foot to the hilltop. He was also frequently checking the red dot on his GPS device. He needed a vantage point to the location thirty-seven degrees north from the hilltop. The sun's position was crucial, and daylight was waning. He checked his earpiece. There was no response from Wick. He could only hope Wick would be at the right place at the right time, before the sunset. Meanwhile, he needed to find his spot.

⎓

Wick looked around and found a marked difference between the village and how he had perceived it to be. They had decorated the path to the marketplace with small blue flags. Once the caravan reached the entry spot, the event organizer came to meet the elders and escorted them to the registration desk. Zahoor moved forward and placed a pile of papers on the desk. The organizer looked satisfied with the documents. He then asked one of his men to show Zahoor and the others the spot reserved for them for the next seven days. Wick remained invisible during all this. He wanted to break free of the group as soon as possible, and he knew he would get a chance soon.

Sure enough, Zahoor and few young people started on the first thing they had to do—erect tents. The rest started to unload their wares. There was a lot to be done and, in the bustle of work, Wick was forgotten.

He secretly checked his watch for the GPS information. Wasim's SUV was a mile to his left. He checked the sun's position and found himself calculating the time left before darkness would descend. There wasn't much time left for him to finish the job. He had to start his journey now.

CHAPTER 19

WASIM CHECKED HIS CASIO F-91W, given to him by Basit. It was a cheap watch, easy to buy anywhere in the world, and it could also work as a handy bomb detonator if needed. But for now, it only marked his depleting patience.

He'd have preferred to simply shoot the American and move on to better things, but his commander had other thoughts.

Basit had gone to meet the Great Cleric at Kandahar. The Cleric's involvement had further complicated what should have been a relatively simple situation. Wasim knew it was above his pay grade and he shouldn't think much about it, yet the sudden interest of the Cleric in their prisoner intrigued him. It didn't help that he had a deep aversion towards the man himself. Wasim didn't approve of the Great Cleric's way of operating. He was slow and indecisive. Maybe it was his age—he was already on the wrong side of fifty.

. . .

The other thing bothering him was the place itself—Division 71, where he was standing.

He abhorred this windowless underground bunker. It literally made his skin crawl. He hated it more than the others. It had the vibe of a mental hospital. Only the attendants here were not like the orderlies in white uniforms.

This place had been refurbished recently. A brainchild of the Great Cleric, it was designed to weaken the human spirit. Wasim did not understand how the handlers who manned this facility and walked these corridors resisted the oppressive claustrophobia and depression this place induced.

From outside, the facility looked like any small one-room hut standing in the middle of ninety acres of barren land. Cattle grazed the vast tracts. Shepherds tended their herds. Maintaining this kind of cover was especially important given the prying eyes of the American satellites that constantly hovered ghost-like over their country. The ruse had worked perfectly so far. No one knew about the shelter's existence. Even the Taliban leadership had no information about its existence. It was completely off the books. The army securing it came from the personal wealth of the Great Cleric, a by-product of his connections in the Pakistani intelligence agency, ISI. The sweet irony was that it was U.S. aid aimed to eliminate terrorism that partly funded the facility.

. . .

It was a relic of an earlier war, one of several sites used by the British in the 1900s to fight against the Afghan tribal armies. Terrible things had been done to people in this crypt. This was where the most notorious Afghan tribal leaders had been tortured and executed to death. People, in fact, had forgotten about it, yet it was now back in use.

It wasn't a pleasant place, but Wasim knew it was a necessary cog in the wheel of fueling rage against America. He knew its significance, but that didn't mean he had to like it.

Wasim looked at the prisoner again. Fletcher was now hanging somewhere between light and dark, his head still, his chin touching his chest.

CHAPTER 20

WICK COVERED THE DISTANCE QUICKLY, continually checking the GPS. In a few hours, the sun would set, and darkness would descend on the plain barren lands making the extraction more difficult than it already was.

Once he was at a safe distance from the facility, he stood casually amidst a roaming flock of sheep whose shepherd was nowhere in the sight. His silenced Beretta and two Ka-Bar blades lay well within his reach in his coat. Pretending to count the sheep, he casually took in his surroundings.

The wooden door of the target house was manned by two men, who were currently cooling their heels on a cot kept just outside the door. A gust of wind lifted their shawls and revealed that both were armed.

. . .

From outside, the facility looked like a village hut made of mud, but Wick knew better. It was just a ploy to hide the concrete chambers underneath from the prying eyes of American satellites.

Wick knew Josh would be facing intense suffering in those underground chambers. How long he could sustain the torture was the critical question. The state he was in would decide the manner of his rescue.

He switched on his mic and whispered to Eddie. "You ready?"

CHAPTER 21

THE SUN GLINTED off the vast tract of sands as Eddie Vicar lay prone in his vantage point, heavily camouflaged, eye to the lens of a .300 Win-Mag sniper rifle, his weapon of choice. His Bible lay on his left. Tracking the scene, sweating his ass off over a hot rock and under tons of sand. Covered with local grass and scrape leaves, it was a fucking hot case. All he had seen since he began his stakeout were minor dirt-devils swirling in the farm-lands some twelve hundred yards away. The dirt tasted like dogshit. He tried to ignore the discomfort as he lay waiting for this chance. His eyes scanned the only wooden gate in the vast desolate land.

At long last, Wick's voice crackled in his earpiece. Time for action. He knew Wick was much closer to the target than he was. His job was to give Wick the best possible entry.

Sand and rocks, goats and shepherds, he blurred everything else out of his vision and focused on the two men sitting on a cot outside the door. The door opened and a third man came out, talking on his cell phone, his hair tossed by the wind.

Eddie keyed the mike and whispered, "I got a new military-age male, talking on a cell phone, standing at the door."

Wick responded, "Got it."

Eddie shifted the rifle's crosshair slightly to the left of the man, compensating for the wind. He inhaled deeply, held, then expelled the air. Sucked in air again. Closed his eyes. The world flooded back in. He felt his breath filling every cell of his body. This was his ritual. Master your breath, master your mind. After that pulling the trigger became an inanimate effort as he exhaled, he tapped his natural respiratory pause and space between his heartbeats. He was trained to kill. The rules were simple—aim for the eye, then you might hit the neck. The worst-case scenario was to aim for the stomach, where you might hit the legs or nothing.

The man with the cell phone looked to his right as if there was something incoming from that direction. Eddie glanced in that direction and paused. An open Toyota was racing towards the hut leaving a trail of dust in its wake.

Wick saw it too. The SUV covered the distance in less than ten minutes and stopped near the door.

. . .

Looking through the scope, Eddie smiled.

CHAPTER 22

"DID YOU NOTICE THE TOYOTA?" **Eddie asked.**

"Yes, but I couldn't get a clear picture of the men in it."

"You will find this interesting."

"What?"

"Abdul Basit has just entered the facility."

"Abdul Basit!" This time even Wick couldn't hide his shock. He was the reason Wick was in Afghanistan for the last five months. Barely a week before his arrival in Kabul, the Taliban had killed seven people in a bomb attack on a police station. The month before, thirty-seven people had died in a Taliban attack on a well-known expat restaurant. Abdul Basit had led both attacks. Officially, he was wanted dead or alive for the several atrocities he had committed, but his true value lay in his knowledge of the key players and plotlines that linked the terror networks of Iraq, Afghanistan, and Pakistan. The TF-77 wanted to get their hands on him, and they needed him alive. Wick had been on Basit's tail for the last several months that had taken him to Pakistan, Iraq and then back to Afghanistan.

But even Abdul Basit was a pawn in the larger scheme of things. He worked for a man called Irfan-Ul-Haq, commonly known as the Great Cleric. Haq was their main target, but being a religious figurehead in Pakistan, there was little they could do about him unless they could piece together enough evidence to unequivocally show his connection with the Taliban. Only Abdul Basit could give them those proofs, and now he was here.

━━━

In the underground facility, Wasim stood watching Josh. He had always considered himself a reasonable man, and he understood that the man sitting on the other side of the mirror could be a hardened professional, ready to die rather than betray his country. But Wasim doubted Josh had ever encountered a ruthless interrogator like Basit.

Basit was an expert in getting the nastiest secrets out of any person. He had once explained his methodology to Wasim - People seldom considered the means necessary to get what they genuinely sought and that was what made them weak and ineffective. Basit focused on what he wanted. The next step was knowing who could provide him with what he wanted, and what he himself needed to do to get it from that person.

If the path to his desires involved causing unthinkable pain to a person so much so that the person begged to be allowed to die, he would not hesitate to do what was required. If it required him to hook alligator clips to a man's balls and send two hundred amperes of searing current through his body or to get a woman gang-raped by his men for days or weeks until she slipped into a coma, Basit had no problem in giving the orders, or in getting his own hands dirty.

People would tell you anything and everything to stop the pain. They would sign anything. Tell you anything you wanted to know. They would even turn against their own mothers. It was monstrous, it was cruel, but Wasim knew people like Basit were required to counter a barbaric nation like America.

Moreover, he had no sympathy for men like Josh. Josh was lying about being a journalist and Wasim hated liars more than anything else. Josh was a CIA dog and Wasim had heard stories of his Taliban brothers being tortured by the agency. This man deserved a gruesome death, but he restrained himself because of his orders.

The door behind him opened and a slightly older man entered the room. His deep black eyes flicked from Wasim to the three fighters in the room. Then, he strode to the two-way mirror, his stance communicating to everyone that he was in charge now.

. . .

Seeing Basit, Wasim's doubts and questions evaporated. He was one of the best in the business and Wasim knew that his presence meant only one thing. The Great Cleric had given his nod to get everything out of the hostage by any means necessary.

Wasim could not help himself but admire how his mentor carried himself. Basit had an air of aloofness about him. His hair was bound in a short ponytail and his cropped beard was perfectly trimmed. He was a Pakistani Muslim, fluent in Urdu, Pashto, Arabic, Farsi, and English. He was dressed in a dark pathani suit, an outfit designed to deliver a sense of authority and influence. His eyes pierced the prisoner with a steely coldness. He had met the prisoner once before, eight hours ago, but this time it was different. His body language showed his determination to break the man.

He had regulated every aspect of every moment of the prisoner's captivity. Every sound, temperature variation, food portion, even the amount of liquid in his body had been meticulously monitored as per his instructions. The ultimate goal was that when the actual torture began, the subject was already on the verge of breaking and would start talking immediately. That saved both time and energy.

The first phase was already in motion. The prisoner had been isolated and stripped of all sense of time and place. by subjecting him to complete sensory deprivation. He was in a state where he would welcome contact of any kind. The second phase was to throw the man a lifeline. Start a dialogue. And the third phase was to raise the tempo.

The job needed a precise thoroughness, time and patience but those were luxuries Basit did not have in this case. He was on a tight schedule and that meant the information had to be extracted quickly and the body dumped.

His orders were crystal clear—get him to talk A.S.A.P.

CHAPTER 23

BASIT GLANCED at Wasim and detected an unspoken glee on the latter's face. He knew his lieutenant was eager to get the action started. He had been twiddling his thumbs for some time now, getting restless all this while.

He motioned towards the door separating the prisoner from them.

Wasim nodded and gazed at the fatigued, chained prisoner. A slow smile played on his lips. He pushed the door open. Josh jerked his head slightly but showed no inclination to see who it was. Basit entered the room with one fighter and closed the door from inside. Wasim returned to his place behind the mirror. The show was about to start, and he had box seats.

Josh Fletcher. A made-up name, most likely. They had checked his ID, and his story of being a journalist checked out, but Basit knew he was not what he seemed. The information he had received was rock solid. All he needed was to get Fletcher to accept that. It had to be done soon. If not, he was worried he would find himself on the wrong side of the cleric and Pakistan's ISI.

The reason was that without informing anyone at the ISI, Basit had ordered Wasim to grab Fletcher and bring him here. The seizure of two of his fighters by the CIA and a growing fear that the USA had begun to tighten its grip on the Afghanistan and Pakistan's terror network had provoked him into acting without authorization. But the kidnapping of an American came with heavy risks. If things didn't go as planned, he had effectively signed his own death warrant. If the word got out about this, all his achievements would be zilch. His contacts would scatter like cockroaches.

His little adventure had gone too far in the last eight hours and he still had no concrete confession or even a shred of useful information. His meeting with the Great Cleric had also not gone well. Even though he had agreed to support Basit by not letting this information slip into the Islamabad power corridors for the next twelve hours, it came with a rider. Basit had to get the hostage to confess his CIA roots in those twelve hours.

The words from the Great Cleric reverberated in his head: "You do not want to test my patience. If you don't have what it takes to get the information, then I can ask Razzaq to take over."

. . .

Basit could not let that happen. He studied the prisoner, thinking hard about how to get to the point as soon as possible.

A good cop, bad cop technique might work. On the right person, the results could be satisfactory. But Josh Fletcher didn't seem to fall in that category.

Basit looked at the glass where he knew Wasim was standing, watching intently, studying his every move. His protégé, his right hand. Now he had to take control of this botched operation in the next few minutes in front of his student to show him how it was done. The time for foreplay was over. He turned back to the prisoner and at that moment, he was ready.

CHAPTER 24

JOSH WAS NUMB. He had no idea how long he had been in that room. All he knew that no one was coming to save him. He suspected that his own colleagues had set him up. From the day he had signed up for this job he had known this day would eventually come. The only thing he regretted was that he could not let the world know what he now knew about his fellow CIA agents. Despite everything, he was certain of one thing—his abductors were not getting anything out from him. His cover was that of a journalist, and he had to stick to that till they either believed him or killed him.

His story and his credentials were his only hope. He was a journalist. He was in Afghanistan for stories on how the common man was coping in a war-torn nation. This gave him an excuse to visit places where no one dared to go, and his press ID card got him through most obstacles he encountered.

· · ·

Though the recent hours were fuzzy in his mind, his recollection of his capture was vivid. Peter, another CIA agent in Afghanistan, had called him to a dilapidated house in Helmand. He was near the place when an open Toyota stopped near him. Two gunmen jumped out of the vehicle and started asking questions. He had faced such questions from the day he had landed in this country, and initially he was not worried. But these people who had accosted him seemed to be looking for something specific in his answers. Something damning. They rummaged through his bag and dumped its contents on the ground. He told himself that the key was to keep his calm. He didn't have to feign the fear he felt, but that was only natural for an innocent journalist who wasn't adept at facing men with AK-47s. But the men were adamant in their belief that he was not a journalist. The more Josh threw his credentials and his articles on the CNN website at them, the more determined they became to prove him wrong.

Then, he played the final card he had, he asked them to call his boss at the CNN. He gave them the number and the email, knowing they would not call, but even if they did, his story would pass muster. He stared at them for a minute but got no response. They seemed confused at the offer. His broken Pashto, combined with hand gestures, was almost successful in getting him out of the trap, but then another Toyota screeched to a halt at the curb and before he could make a move, they dragged him into it. His mouth was gagged, his hands cuffed, and his head covered with a black hood. He had apparently passed out, and when he opened his eyes, he was in a semi-dark room, sitting on a broken chair, his hands cuffed behind his back. Over the next few hours, he was tortured and beaten, even as he battled a raging thirst.

. . .

He sensed that his endgame was near. He was going to die in this dank cell.

CHAPTER 25

BASIT WATCHED as Josh buckled over in the chair and crashed to the ground. He hit the concrete deck hard but didn't try to get up. Basit had seen people in this hopeless situation innumerable times. He knew the prisoner's condition was futile.

Basit signaled one of the two men standing in opposite corners of the room to straighten the hostage up and to remove the cuffs.

The fighter threw a glass of water at the prisoner's face and pulled him into a sitting position on the chair. Josh came to his senses and found his hands free. He rubbed his wrists, first the right and then the left, where the cuffs had been a few seconds ago. He looked up at his interrogator.

Basit handed him a glass of water which Josh accepted with no change in his expression.

.   .   .

The Taliban minion went back to his position in the corner. The other one was already in position.

"Josh," Basit said in understandable English, "I want to start this all over again."

Josh glared at his interrogator with inflamed eyes and parroted his lines again, "I am telling the truth. I am a journalist with CNN, you can call my boss and confirm it."

Basit took a deep breath and his words came out in a measured tone, "I told you I want to start over again. You need to think about your options very carefully. The way I see it, your country has left you to die. It's been twenty-four hours, and no one is looking for you. You are not missed by anyone." He paused again. The timeline was a lie, but he knew Josh had no way of knowing. They had kept him sedated for the most part of his captivity, and in that underground room there was no sense of time.

Josh remained silent, trying to call the bluff of his interrogator. He knew that in any abduction the first twenty-four hours carried the best chance of rescue. Had it really been a day since he had been taken? He suspected Basit was lying, but had no way of knowing.

.   .   .

"You know your country's policy—they say do not negotiate with people like us. That means only one thing—they disowned you the moment you were captured." He signaled to one of his men, who exited the room. When he came back, he was pushing a table on wheels. Josh glanced at it. Alligator clips attached to a battery. He knew what those meant, but he didn't know if he was ready.

"I am telling you," Josh was firm, "I have nothing to offer you. Damn it, I am just a bloody journalist." He emphasized the word journalist.

"You still think they will come for you." Basit laughed hard, very hard. It was an act, but he was an expert and everyone watching him was convinced the thought had really amused him.

Josh knew reacting was useless. It was a rhetorical question. He glanced at the clips from the corner of his eyes. Basit saw no fear in his eyes. He wasn't a journalist. Journalists fear alligator clips.

"Okay Mr. Fletcher, if you want to play games with me, I'll play along too. Let's be clear, though, all this can be made to stop if you choose. It's you who is making me do it." Basit picked up the clips.

The two minions in the room stepped forward. Basit looked at the mirror and, on his cue, a third man entered the room. Two of them held Josh down by his arms while the third held his legs in a firm grip, immobilizing him completely from neck down.

CHAPTER 26

WICK LOOKED at the sky again, and then at the door. The three men outside stood in a triangular formation—two in front, one behind—which indicated some level of training.

Wick had no idea how many more men were inside. All he had was an element of surprise on his side and he wanted to keep it that way. These men had no inkling that he was there. Their confidence would be their Achilles' heel.

"Eddie, I'm going in. Your turn now," he whispered.

Eddie checked Wick's position through the lens. He was creeping closer to the door. The three gunmen paid him no heed. They weren't expecting any surprises. Not from a shepherd anyway.

.   .   .

Wick was one of the few people whom Eddie trusted to do this kind of job. His confidence was because of two things. First, Wick, like himself, put his life on the line, never shying away from getting his hands dirty in the field. Second, Eddie had seen him in action, and he was efficient, ruthlessly efficient. In fact, he was the best Eddie had ever seen in this trade.

Wick knew Eddie would do his job. Belying his macho call sign 'Bear', Eddie was barely five-foot-four and weighed just about one hundred and fifty pounds, but what he lacked in size he made up for in talent. He was one of the best snipers in open spaces and even better in urban conditions. And with that reputation came respect. Other fighters tended to give snipers a wide berth. Their survival instincts told them it wasn't a good idea to mess with someone who could shoot you dead from a thousand yards.

"Great. I was beginning to wonder when we would get this thing rolling," he said into his mike.

"Start the countdown on my mark," Wick whispered.

Eddie packed a dip. Loaded bullets in the wrist-sheath. Marshaled his breath again.

He heard Wick's voice in the earpiece. "Three, two, one, mark."

.   .   .

Time slowed as he lowered his eye to the lens. He pulled the trigger. The bullet leaped from the barrel, cracking like a whip. The .300 round hurled forward, glinting as it entered the flesh of the man standing one step back in the triangle of guards.

CHAPTER 27

THE ROOM ECHOED with Josh's screams. The electric charge ran through the alligator clips to his testicles and to then through his entire body.

Wasim smiled, watching from outside. Basit was just as relentless as he had imagined.

"Mr. Fletcher, I know this might be uncomfortable for you, but my God has given me the permission to send Kafirs to their hell. Being a religious man, I have to do what he wants from me." Basit tilted his head, talking to Josh over his incessant screams. "Are you not a religious person, Mr. Fletcher? Don't you have any sympathy for the people killed by your government? I ask you again, very politely, help me help you."

Josh barely had time to catch his breath before another round of current seared through his body.

. . .

"I'm sure you understand that you have left me with no other option," continued a sneering Basit. "No one is coming to save you. Why do you want to die in this chamber for men who have betrayed you and a country that has forgotten you?" There was no malice in his voice as he said this, merely regret.

Another round of current wracked Josh's body.

Josh wandered in and out of consciousness, his mind straying to his home and Natalie, his wife. She was waiting for him, her husband, who was in the most dangerous country in the world, especially for an American citizen.

"Why do you have to take this project?" Natalie had demanded when he had told her he would be away for two months on an assignment near the Af-Pak border. "CNN can send someone else. You're just back from Iraq and now this." She had been on the verge of crying, her blue eyes filled with concern for him.

Josh lifted his head and stared past the bright light at his interrogator. His eyes were pleading. "Please talk to my boss," he gasped. "Ask them. They will tell you I am just a low-key journalist."

Basit shook his head. "Your superiors have forsaken you. You are nothing but a plague to them. They claim to know nothing about what you've been up to."

"You are lying," spat Fletcher.

This was exactly what Basit was after. Mood swings, uncontrollable and sudden. Desperate and pleading one second, angry and antagonistic the next. He raised his hands in a gesture of helplessness. "I have been very patient with you, and all you do in return is feed me more lies and insults."

"I am telling you the truth!" Josh said it far too quickly.

Basit gave him an almost caring look. "Will you tell your God that I have been good to you?" He pushed the switch once again. Josh's body shivered violently.

⊏⊐

The storm was closing in. Josh two-stepped Natalie around the dance floor to George Michael's romantic "Careless Whispers." He looked youthful and dapper, and she was flush with grace and optimism. Both had always wanted a quiet wedding. And today they basked in each other's embrace.

CHAPTER 28

THE BULLET HIT the left eye of the man standing one step back among the three fighters. His deadweight hit the wall behind with a dull thud.

The man standing to his right turned first. By the time he could figure out what had happened, his colleague was already dead. He whirled around, his grip tightening on his gun, his finger trigger-ready. Unhesitant to kill the enemy.

Eddie adjusted the crosshairs over his next target. Another blast of sand. Another crack of the whip. The .300 round sped forward, eager to meet its target.

It hit the left side of its victim's skull, even as the man was getting ready to fire. He hit the dirt, spewing blood. The only man left looked left and right, trying desperately to locate the shooter.

He saw a figure approaching him, and his instinct was to drop his cell phone and raise his gun.

Wick was now sprinting, his Berretta out. Two 9mm bullets left the silenced barrel and found the center of his target's forehead. The third fighter died on the spot with shock in his eyes. He hadn't even got a chance to lift his gun.

Three men down in less than fifteen seconds and not a sound to warn the others inside.

CHAPTER 29

BASIT WOULD NOT BACK DOWN. Not now that he had sensed an opening. The man would talk, and soon.

"Let me ask you, Josh, would you like to see your family?

Josh was exhausted and in extreme pain. His gaze dropped to the floor, and he tried to think straight. He didn't want to pursue any conversation with his tormentor.

"My men have been kind to you since you've been here. You think they cannot break you?" Basit grabbed Fletcher's jaw and forced his face towards him.

Josh stared into Basit's eyes and recognized a sense of satisfaction. Basit was not done with Josh. Far from it. If Josh thought this was the end, he was very wrong. This was just the beginning.

"You think we are weak. We cannot break your CIA training. You are wrong. From now on, things change. You can lie to me no more. You insult me no more with your phony stories. From here on, things are going to get messy."

"I am telling you the truth," Josh screamed and stretched out to touch his interrogator's arm.

Basit caught him midway and pressed a nerve. Josh's screams magnified. His eyes pleaded with Basit to leave him alone. Finally, Basit released his wrist and left the room. His men followed him out.

CHAPTER 30

BASIT CAME out of the room. He knew that making someone wait in dread, wondering what would come next, was as effective a means of torture as anything physical. He waited outside the room, watching Josh in silence, letting the tension build. Wasim stood a step behind, looking at him in admiration.

For a few minutes, Josh remained still. And then he slowly began to unravel. Over the next five minutes, he shook violently, cried and looked around desperately for a way to escape. The transformation happened rapidly. His panicky movements rocked the chair and he lost his balance again, hitting the floor hard. He tried to crawl to the safety of the nearest corner. But he had no strength. He was in deep pain and his lower body was almost useless.

Basit knew the shocks had done their job—half of Fletcher's body was numb and some of his body parts may never work again, and yet he was still alive. Basit had not hit him, he had not even touched him. The only thing he had done was to attach the clips to his gonads, and they had done everything else.

Josh grew more and more troubled by the second, dragging his lifeless naked body on the floor, seeking whatever safety he could find in that small room. The door opened again and Basit came back in. The look on Josh's face was of sheer horror.

Basit snarled looking at Josh, "I have given you enough time. Now, I will ask only one question and if you lie..." he gestured towards his companions, "they will break your bones, one at a time, a bone for every lie."

Josh looked at them in terror. He knew Basit was not bluffing.

"Who do you work for?"

"CNN."

Basit nodded at one of the men, who held Josh's arm down on the seat of the wrecked chair. The other raised his heavy boot and came down hard on it. With a loud snap, the arm was broken. Josh screamed.

"Who do you work for?"

. . .

"Please..." Josh gasped. "No... please..."

Basit put his boot on top of the broken arm and pressed down. Josh screamed in agony.

Basit snarled, "I'm not taking my foot off until you answer me!"

Josh kept screaming.

"Who do you work for?"

"CNN! CNN!" The man's face was covered in sweat and contorted in anguish.

"I told you not to lie to me," Basit said, speaking slowly, menacingly.

"I swear I'm telling you the truth!" Josh gasped.

Another signal and, this time, it was the other arm. The pain shot up a hundred-fold. Tears flooded Josh's eyes and ran down his face. His head was throbbing. His arms lay limp and bleeding at his sides. He tried to crawl away, using his face and chest to move forward. Anything to get away from the butchers.

.   .   .

Basit drew a letter-sized manila envelope from his back pocket and retrieved a photo from it. He threw it on the floor beside Josh. "Does she look familiar?" And he began to roll up his sleeves.

Josh looked at the photo through bleary eyes. He knew who the person in the picture was, but he also knew it was perilous to accept that. He shook his head weakly.

CHAPTER 31

A POWERFUL BLAST of hot wind hit Wick, smacking his flowing outfit against his body. Wick lowered his head and squinted through the sand and dust but didn't slacken his pace. The third guard had barely hit the ground when he was at the door. A hundred yards covered in seconds. The sun was setting in the west. Ballooning clouds crowded the evening sky.

Wick knew Eddie was watching his every move. The assurance that someone had his back was enough for him to take the plunge. His run ended at the closed door. He stood amidst three dead bodies, his back against the wall. Looking in Eddie's direction, he gave a thumbs-up sign. Wick understood that those two shots by Eddie were nothing short of a miracle. Without those impossible shots, they wouldn't have stood a chance. And now it was his turn.

Leaning against the mud wall, Wick closed his eyes for a moment. He focused on his breathing, visualizing what was to come.

Enter the bunker. Use the blade. No sound. He opened his eyes and tapped his coat, feeling the reassuring bulges of the Ka-Bar and the three Beretta magazines. His chest tightened at the thought of what he was about to do. A little anxiety is always good.

Wick had no idea how many people he would find inside. He was going in completely blind. His life rested on his skills and his luck. Nothing else mattered.

"I'm going in. The connection might not be so good inside so stay put and wait for thirty minutes before making a move." Wick said to Eddie. He shrugged off his coat and took out the Ka-Bar.

Eddie checked his watch, then whispered. "Best of luck, brother. I'll be here."

Wick grinned hearing his voice and then slowly pulled the door open. From the crack, he saw stairs descending into the darkness. He checked the time, took a deep breath, and glanced once in Eddie's direction before disappearing inside the hut.

CHAPTER 32

THE STAIRS WENT STRAIGHT DOWN, then took a sharp left turn. It was semi-dark, and Wick paused for a moment to adjust his vision. He listened hard for footsteps. Nothing. There was no movement on the stairs. Once his vision had adjusted, he descended the stairs, careful not to make any sound. Heels first, toes next.

The cramped space gave him little space to maneuver should someone come upon him. He had no option but to cover the distance as fast as he could without making a noise. At the bend, he stopped, listening for any sound from the other side. Nothing. He then took out a tiny cam attached to a foldable wire to a small round screen. Dropping to a squat at the last step of the stairs, he slowly extended the cam to check the other side of the bend. Six more steps, and then a concrete floor that could be seen only in patches, mostly where it was cracked and jutted upward. The rest of the floor was covered with a matted layer of sand and dirt.

. . .

Wick took a moment to examine his surroundings, then walked through the corridor to the first door. It was shut. He put his ear against it. Silence. He carefully twisted the handle anticlockwise. The door opened, without creaking. Wick leaned in and checked the room.

Clear.

To his right, ten feet ahead, he saw light spilling into the hallway from an open room. Wick paused and wiped his palms. Took a step. Tested the floor. No sound. He marched ahead, staying close to the wall. He halted an arm's length shy of the lighted room. Took a deep breath.

His grip on the Ka-Bar tightened. He had learned to use it in missions with the Joint Task Force 2. It was a weapon useful for self-defense and in knife fights. The grip fitted the hand so perfectly that it was very difficult to disarm anyone holding one.

He peeked inside. Two men seated side by side, their backs towards the door, their rifles carelessly propped against the wall. Wick slipped in noiselessly to see a wall lined with several screens showing CCTV footage from within the facility. He peered at the screen. It was Josh, the man from the file. Crawling and bleeding on the floor. Looking for a way out. The screens were muted but Wick could see that Josh was screaming in pain.

. . .

Wick looked sideways and took a long silent step into the room. Paused. Held his breath. Reversed the knife in his hand, blade outward. Raised his arm, cocked it behind the first militant's head and closed the loop with a snap. The knife buried itself six inches deep in the back of terrorist's neck.

The terrorist's body went rigid in response to the unanticipated assault. He arched his back and his mouth opened wide to let loose a scream of agony, but Wick was too quick, too well trained in the art of efficient killing. His free hand moved from the militant's shoulder to his mouth, stifling the cry. He quickly drew the knife out.

The other terrorist turned at the slight sound, but Wick's hand was already in motion. The terrorist pushed himself away from the table, half-rising. Wick watched him calculate the distance between himself and his rifle. The man looked unsure about the best manner to salvage the situation but finally, he went for the gun.

Wick's knuckles hardened, and he sidestepped to give himself more room to take an accurate swing. The man blinked, and Wick landed his left punch on his Adam's apple. The terrorist's hand recoiled back and grabbed his neck, gagging. With his right hand, Wick swung the Ka-Bar, and it hit the jugular vein through the man's fingers. Blood leaked from the puncture. The gag now turned into silent screams.

. . .

Wick cut his throat, ear to ear. Then he turned back and cut the first soldier's throat, too. Just in case. Blood soaked the table-top, dripping to the floor. It didn't spurt, just leaked. Wick squatted and wiped the blade clean on the dead soldier's shirt.

CHAPTER 33

THEY NEVER KNEW what hit them. Wick ejected the magazines from the two assault rifles and hid them behind the TV screens. He checked the screens. One showed an armed man assaulting Josh who was on the ground. Even as he watched, the man almost casually broke Josh's right leg with his boot. The prisoner's agony could be felt even through the silent screen.

The scene would have been disturbing to anyone, but its effect on Wick was especially profound. His face had taken on a very strange look, eyes narrowed into slits, jaw tight, sweat on his forehead. It seemed almost as if he were metamorphosing into someone else.

Wick shook his head several times, muttering expletives under his breath, his teeth clenched. A fierce battle raged within him. The logical side of his brain told him he must save Josh by sticking to the plan. He knew it was his sane voice, the one he should listen to, yet there was another voice in his head that was telling him something entirely different.

He forced himself to calm down. All his professional training had taught him he should stay on course and continue to hunt down the enemy one by one without revealing his presence. His job was to make Basit talk, get Josh out alive and blow up the facility.

Four people in the room along with Josh. Two dead bodies here and three outside. This meant Wick knew about nine positions. What about the rest? His survival depended on finding them before they found him.

He exited the room, closing the door gently behind him. The corridor was still deserted. He crept to the next room; it was empty. He continued carefully down the corridor. Suddenly, a fighter in military fatigues stepped out into the hallway right in front of him. The man froze momentarily in shock, finding a stranger in the corridor. Before his hand could go to the Kalashnikov strung across his shoulder, Wick's Ka-Bar rose and sliced down, jabbing the man in the throat. Wick buried the blade deep in his neck and jerked it left, severing the windpipe while stepping aside to avoid the spray of blood. He caught the semi-dead body by the shirt as it fell and dragged it back into the room the man had just come out of. It was a weapons store, with a table and chair at the center. Wick bent down and clamped the man's head between his hands, twisted it left and then jerked it right. The neck broke with a snap that was loud but not loud enough to worry about. Still, Wick froze, listening hard for approaching footsteps. Sixty seconds later, a movement in the corridor caught his attention and he withdrew his Beretta and swung it in that direction. He moved slowly towards the door, letting the sound of the footsteps come closer. The militant walked down the corridor like he was in no hurry. He crossed the armory room. Wick, from his crouched sitting position in the shadows, saw the distinct outline of a man with a Kalashnikov strung across his body armor. The man's back was towards him. Wick waited for him to approach. He put his Beretta on the ground very carefully and got to his feet. His blade was back in his hand. At the threshold of the room, he stopped and looked at the other side of the corridor. They were alone. Closing the distance between him and the militant, he quickly got into position.

The militant sensed his presence and whirled around. His eyes met Wick even as the blade pierced his soft belly. The militant's hands grabbed Wick's attacking hand. His mouth opened to scream but Wick's free hand covered his mouth tightly shoving him against the wall. The man squirmed, pinned against the wall, but Wick turned the knife's handle first clockwise, then anti-clockwise, and then withdrew it. The man instinctively covered the knife wound with both hands. His legs gave way, but Wick kept him pinned against the wall. The militant raised his right leg and started banging the wall behind to call for help.

Wick's hand rose to his prey's neck and severed his right jugular vein, spraying blood.

It had an immediate impact on the man who stopped wriggling. A shudder went through him and then his lifeless body collapsed forward on Wick.

.   .   .

Wick quickly dragged the body into the same room where a minute ago he had hidden the other dead militant. He picked up his Berretta from the floor and stepped out of the room, pivoting to the opposite side of the corridor, his eyes scanning the area.

There!

Another militant lurked at the far end of the corridor. And, like his fallen friend, he hadn't seen Wick. But his head was cocked. He had possibly heard a noise. The man knew something was amiss but was still unsure what it was. The militant was looking for movement and Wick intended to give him what he wanted. He took out his second blade. His knife-wielding hand suddenly lashed out. The blade shot through the air. The militant heard the whooshing sound, but before he could determine the source, the Ka-bar blade dug hard into his left cheek. The man's head jerked backwards, and he stumbled. Dropping his gun, he instinctively pressed both palms against the left side of his face to alleviate the pain. That's when he heard footsteps approaching. From the corner of his eye, he saw a silhouette approaching him. The man needed help. He tried opening his mouth but couldn't. The effort caused the knife to dig further into his face. All he could manage was a feeble gagging sound. The second Ka-Bar in Wick's right hand arrived a second later and with one snap it pierced his Adam's apple.

His arms went stiff. His body fell against door behind. The door banged hard against the wall. Dead before Wick blinked.

. . .

One more down.

Wick paused and listened, strangely there wasn't any movement in the corridor. No one was coming for him, at least not yet. But he knew someone would, soon. The door had made quite a noise.

He dragged the body of the dead militant back into the room from where he had come and set it on the chair in a sitting position, head on the table. Anyone glancing in from the corridor would see a man grabbing a quick shuteye. Wick then sandwiched himself between the door and wall. He slowed down his breathing to a minimum, calming his mind. He left the door open, the feeble light from the room, spilling into the corridor.

He heard soft footsteps approaching.

A door not far from him opened. A man was in the corridor but on the opposite side, away from where Wick was. Wick concentrated on his footsteps. The soft sound was measured, as if the man was scoping the area in a hunched position. The steps stopped at the threshold of the room. Wick could hear him breathing on the other side of the door. So, the man on the other side could probably also hear Wick. He slowed his breathing. Wick had unknowingly put himself in a very precarious situation. And he was in no position to respond. Even a junked AK-47 could easily tear down a hundred such wooden doors. If it came to that it had only one ending—Wick's death. His life right then was hanging on a very thin thread of luck.

The militant stayed at the door for a few seconds longer, gazing at his colleague. The dim light was making it difficult to ascertain anything.

"Aslam! You okay?"

Aslam didn't respond. The militant rushed towards the table. Wick saw the back of his new target, AK-47 in his right hand. He slowly came out from the shadows and positioned himself right behind his new target. And then he did something unexpected.

"Everything okay?" he asked his target in Arabic.

"Aslam is dead," the man responded, turning around, his gun still slack at his side. As soon as he turned fully, Wick's hands shot upwards and two Ka-Bars pierced the man's soft skin between his Adam's apple and his jaws on both sides. The upward thrust of the Cro-van steel blades was such that the militant was momentarily in the air. His body shivered violently, then went limp. Wick slowly lowered him onto the table behind him, careful not to make a sound.

Another man down.

CHAPTER 34

THERE WERE STILL a few rooms left to be checked. The stuffy wind had made him lose his stamina a lot faster than under normal circumstances. He needed water urgently. He looked around in the room. No water. His tongue was dry and almost white. He couldn't even wet his lips. But he couldn't risk losing the momentum. He still had to be ultra-careful in checking each of the remaining rooms.

The next three rooms gave him no surprises. But no water either in any of those rooms.

It finally came down to the last two rooms.

Basit was in one of those rooms. With the Ka-Bar in his left hand, Wick proceeded with caution. The penultimate room was empty. He didn't waste much time there. He had to move faster now; the finish line was closer.

.   .   .

The door of the last room was slightly open. Inside, was a two-way mirror behind which was unfolding the same scene he had seen on the TV screen in the guard room. Five men in total. One stood on Wick's side of the mirror, watching the other four who were on the other side; one of the four was Abdul Basit. They were all looking at someone on the floor. Wick knew it was Josh, though he couldn't say if he was dead or alive.

Wick decided to focus on the man standing on his side of the mirror, his back towards him, engrossed in watching the torture through the glass. No one on the other side would know when Wick killed him; he only had to be silent.

The other thing he noticed was that the room was soundproofed, unlike any other room he had seen so far in the facility, and that explained why the sounds had not alerted them.

Pushing the door open further, he stepped in quietly, checking both sides to make sure no one else was in the room. He approached Wasim from behind, his pace measured, his steps silent, heel first, followed by the rest of the foot.

His blade clutched in his left hand, with fluid precision, he grabbed Wasim's hair with his right and yanked his head back. His left hand moved at the same time and the tip of the knife went into the man's neck and then thrust upwards. Six inches of steel sliced through the windpipe and penetrated deep into the base of the brain. With a forceful twist of the blade, the fragile brain stem was torn.

Still holding his hair, Wick lowered Wasim's lifeless body on the floor, careful not to make any noise.

CHAPTER 35

LEAVING Wasim's body in a pool of blood, Wick put his knife back in its place, took out the Beretta and checked the magazine. There was only a thin wall between him and the last four. Yet, he had the advantage of being able to see them, while they could not. There were no guns inside. They had gone inside unarmed as though showing their strength against a helpless prisoner would prove their masculinity. All his earlier feelings came back with force, and his jaw clenched.

He kicked the wood hard and the door opened with a loud crack. Almost instantly, the first bullet burned through the head of the man standing at the farthest corner and emerged from the other side of his skull.

The second guard was shot in the neck. His attempt to scream resulted in more blood from his mouth. He hit the ground hard, still alive, but Wick knew he wouldn't amount to much. Abdul

Basit and his only companion whirled around, but not before Wick fired again, and the third militant's head exploded.

Basit stood frozen amidst the carnage.

CHAPTER 36

"SIT," Wick ordered Basit.

There was no response. Basit remained on his feet observing Wick. Something had dawned on him. He would not get out of here alive. The man in front of him was a trained killer. The evidence was in front of him, drowning in a pool of blood. But he wasn't going to cave in so easily. Quite unexpectedly, he leaped at his attacker.

The move took Wick by surprise. The dead bodies on the floor hindered his movement. Basit aimed his right fist at his enemy's face as he came down on him. Wick tried to deflect the incoming punch and almost lost his grip on his gun in the process.

Basit had put little thought into technique or balance. Most of the punches he had thrown in recent years had been at men tied to a chair or strung up. His street-fighting skills were not what they had once been, so when his target blocked his swing with an awkward step, his power was spent for nothing. His right foot landed on the arm of a dead body and he lost his balance.

Wick was now in control in this impromptu fist fight. He took a steady step forward sidestepping the cadavers. His punch came in at lightning speed and hardened knuckles connected with Basit's nose. A bone-splitting crack sent Basit careening off his feet. The pain blinded him, and he covered his face with both palms.

Wick took the opportunity to quickly crouch beside Josh and check his pulse. He was still alive. He then grabbed the militant who was still breathing by the collar, dragged him over the bodies and dropped him next to Basit.

He then pulled his Beretta's hammer back into the cocked position and leveled it at the militant's knee. Without a question or word of warning, he squeezed the trigger.

Before Basit could react, Wick brought the weapon to bear on him and fired again. Basit's right knee shattered.

The entire thing happened in less than a second, with both men bent over screaming in pain but unable to clutch their shattered kneecaps.

. . .

Wick stepped over the dead bodies and looked down at the two agonized faces. "You didn't really think it was going to be that easy, did you?"

Through his clenched jaw, Basit's eyes still had the same defiance. The militant, on the other hand just lay there on the dirty floor and whimpered to himself.

Wick lowered his weapon and said, "So tell me about the abduction."

"No," Basit yelled with everything he had.

Looming over the two men, Wick reacted instantly and without malice. He grabbed the militant by the hair and shoved his face next to Basit's. He extended his gun and pointed it at the head of the militant. The men had their faces pressed tightly together. Wick pulled the trigger and sent a hollow-tipped bullet into the militant's face. His entire body convulsed at impact and then settled, with only his fingers twitching. Basit was left gasping for air, his eyes stinging from the muzzle blast and his face covered with blood and flesh.

"So," Wick straddled Basit and pointed the barrel at his head. "You and I were talking."

.   .   .

Basit's face contorted in pain from the gunshot to his knee. He looked over at the twitching hand of his dead comrade. A second later he shut his eyes and said, "I cannot tell you anything."

Wick brought his gun up. He would not kill Basit, at least not yet, but the man did not need to know that. "Listen very carefully to me. If you don't tell me everything I want to know, I'm going to kill you, and then I'm going to track down your entire family and kill them. I'll kill your father, your mother, your two wives. I'll kill your five sons. I'll kill your two daughters. I'll then find everyone who is related to you and I'll kill them, too." Wick leaned over, placing the hard steel of the Beretta against his temple and forcing his head onto the dirty floor.

Wick removed the pistol from his temple and shoved it into his groin. "…But first, I'm going to blow your balls off, if you don't start speaking now!"

"Don't shoot! Please." the man pleaded. His face wet with tears.

"Why did you abduct him?"

"I got information from one of my sources that he was a CIA agent."

. . .

"Who?"

"An undercover CIA agent stationed in Kandahar." Wick swallowed his surprise and maintained a neutral expression.

"Names?"

"I don't know, but I have their photos in a flash drive."

"Where is it?"

"My locket."

Wick snatched the locket without mercy.

"Who else is in on this?"

"I don't know the last names of the others. Only their first names. Not sure if it's their real identity."

"Leave that to me to decide."

"Peter, Matt, Scott, Anthony, Allen and Cody."

. . .

"This is their side of the bargain, what about yours?"

"Cocaine and cash every week for intel on the CIA's next move."

"Why him?" Wick indicated Josh's prone figure.

"He wasn't a part of the deal but then he got suspicious about them and started to dig further."

"So, you abducted him to kill him?"

"The plan was to abduct him and then hand his dead body to the CIA. This would set an example for others."

"Clearing the way for your small arrangement. Who ordered the kidnapping?"

"I did."

"What about the Great Cleric? What's his role?"

Basit hesitated and immediately regretted it when a bullet hissed from the Beretta and drilled into his other knee. The pain was worse than death.

. . .

He screamed with all his strength, his blood mixing with that of the dead.

"What is the Cleric planning?" Wick was relentless.

"I don't know. I only know that he is the link between the ISI and Taliban and takes care of the assets in Afghanistan, providing them with the rations, weapons, and intel." Basit gasped out, between heaving sobs.

"I asked, what is he planning?"

"I don't know."

Wick raised his Beretta again.

"Wait… please wait. Don't shoot. I'll tell you. There is an attack planned on America."

Wick showed no reaction. He wanted an unfiltered version from him, without leading him where Wick wanted him to go.

. . .

"When?"

"Today."

"Today? Where?"

"I don't know. He didn't share that information with me."

"Bullshit!"

"I swear I don't know. All I've been told is that they are targeting many cities."

"What cities?"

"I don't know."

"Is it a bomb attack?"

"Yes."

"Nuclear?"

.   .   .

"I don't know."

"Where are the bombs right now?"

"I don't know."

"Wrong answer!" Wick stepped forward. Basit crawled into a corner just as Josh had attempted earlier. Wick swung a kick that fell on Basit like a sledgehammer. He hit the wall. Stunned, Basit threw up his hands to block the next blow.

This time Wick grabbed him by the throat and, even though his opponent was some thirty pounds heavier, he yanked him off the floor and slammed him against the wall like he was a puppet. "Tell me, do you really want to live to see your family?"

Basit croaked, "Live. Live. I want to live."

"Then you'd better get smart fast." Wick threw him on the floor and circled around him, his left fist clenched, his Beretta pointed at his face. "Now, I will only ask you this one last time. What's the plan?"

Wick stared down menacingly at the man and watched in silence as Basit wept. Through sniffles and sobs, he pleaded, "Please... I beg of you, I will tell you everything, but do not hurt me."

. . .

Wick's face twisted into a grimace of disgust. "I am listening."

"Multiple attacks... different cities... same time. The cleric... is working for a man called... P... Professor."

"Professor?"

"No one knows who he is... but he has money and means."

Professor. Wick had heard this name before. He had that email still in his inbox that he had received after his Venezuelan mission about his parents and their connection with a man called the Professor. For the last several months he had found nothing about his family or about this man. Now hearing it again made his head spin. The connection was eerie, and he was in there somewhere in the middle.

Wick knew Basit had a lot more to offer but there wasn't any time. He needed to immediately get this information to Helms. Helms was in a position to alert others. He checked his earpiece. Still no connection.

"Where is the cleric right now?" he asked his last question.

. . .

"Kart-e-Parwan, Kabul." Basit parroted out the address.

Wick knew what that address was—Pakistan's consulate in Afghanistan.

CHAPTER 37

EDDIE CHECKED HIS WATCH. It was eighteen minutes since Wick had disappeared behind that door. As they both had suspected, comms did not work from inside the fortified bunker, so Eddie had no option other than to wait. He checked his earpiece for the tenth time and caught only continuous static.

He looked again through the lens; the coast was clear. Based on his mental calculations, Wick should come out any minute now.

Five minutes later, he heard the static diminishing and a voice rising above it. He plugged his earphone again and heard Wick.

"Eddie, can you hear me?"

"Loud and clear."

. . .

"How is the situation outside?"

Eddie surveyed the area once more through the glass. "Clear."

"I am coming out. Josh is with me. He is injured."

"I'm covering you."

The wooden door opened, and Wick stumbled out, supporting Josh on his left shoulder, the Beretta in his right hand.

He made for the open Toyota in which Basit had arrived. Wick had grabbed the keys from Basit.

Wick put Josh on the passenger seat and switched on the ignition.

"Eddie, I am going inside again. Watch him for me."

"Okay," Eddie whispered.

Wick went straight to the last room and retrieved Basit. He flung his unconscious body on the back seat before disappearing again inside the hut, this time to the weapon store. He checked the shelves and found a crate of grenades along with a canister of flammable kerosene oil. He took the crate and carried it to the turn of the staircase.

He then went back, grabbed the canister and splashed the flammable liquid on the floor of the corridor. He returned to the stairs and took out a grenade. As he exited the hut, he yanked its pin and threw it back at the crate of explosives, closing the door behind him.

Running towards the Toyota, he hopped into the driver's seat and pressed hard on the accelerator. The four-wheeler growled and shot forward. Wick changed gears and drove straight with maximum speed.

Multiple blasts started to rock the terrain. In the rear-view mirror, Wick watched the bunker crumple to the ground. The shock waves rocked the four-wheeler and Wick thought for a moment that the SUV would tumble sideways. But he kept the accelerator floored and the SUV zoomed away. Through the earpiece, Wick could hear Eddie gathering his things.

If Basit had been telling the truth, then Wick needed an urgent talk with Helms, but first, they needed to get to safety.

CHAPTER 38

WICK FINISHED the bottle that was in the Ford while intermittently speaking to Helms. Wick was careful not to reveal his connection with the Professor while revealing the information he had received. He needed more time to establish his link with the name.

Helms listened to Wick without interrupting. He was happy that his assets and Josh were breathing. The information on the rogue agents and cash for intel was alarming, but the pressing concern was the attack.

"How many bombs are we talking about?" asked Helms.

"Basit didn't know it, but I don't trust him. We need more time to grill him," answered Wick.

. . .

"Why can't we go and extract the cleric?" Eddie asked.

"That won't matter for now. If what Basit is telling is true, then the attacks can start any time today." Wick said.

"How much damage?" asked Helms.

"That's contingent on whether we're looking at an air burst or ground detonation, and if it's detonated during the middle of the day or in the evening and how many cities. Immediate casualties could be in thousands," Wick said.

An uncomfortable silence fell over the group as everyone grappled with the enormity of the possible carnage. Eddie uttered a soft curse.

"We don't even know the type of bombs," Helms said. "My team is notifying the FBI and CIA."

"Any response from them yet?"

"FBI—yes. CIA—no, as of now," Helms said.

"Dammit," Wick muttered.

. . .

"What do you want us to do?" Eddie asked.

"Get Josh to the army medical facility in Helmand. Get Basit here. We need to drill him further. A plane will be waiting for you at the air base. I am going to talk to the President," Helms said.

"I hope he doesn't do something stupid," Eddie muttered just before the line was disconnected.

CHAPTER 39

HELMS PICKED up the phone and called the White House Chief of Staff.

"I need to talk to the President."

"Who's this?"

Helms clenched his fists. This was outrageous. Time was running out and the White House Chief of Staff apparently didn't even have his number.

"William Helms—Director of the NSA. Get me the President, this is an emergency."

. . .

"The president is on his way for a game of golf with the President of North Korea. You will have to wait for it to finish."

"Listen, you piece of shit, either you get me the President right now or I will make sure that your career is over before today ends." Helms thundered.

The White House Chief of Staff sniggered at the attempt at bullying him. "The President has specifically asked me to keep morons like you away from him, so you can try, but I think it will be you who will be facing the ax."

This was unprecedented in all of Helms' career. The President had asked his minions to block calls from the NSA director! He saw no point in arguing with the gatekeeper. He needed someone with a sound mind and the authority to act. He disconnected the call.

His next call was to the United States Secretary of Homeland Security. His personal assistant took the call and promised her boss would get back to Helms soon.

Helms then tried Raborn twice, only to have his call disconnected twice. Helms was getting the feeling he was fighting a lonely battle, but he had to keep trying. His next call was to the United States Secretary of Defense, Patrick Mattis, who answered on the third ring.

.   .   .

"Hello Bill, how are you?" Mattis sounded chirpy.

"We have a situation. My sources in Afghanistan have intel about an attack on American soil today. The president is incommunicado. You need to take this to him and request an urgent meeting. I am flying to DC in thirty minutes."

"Bill, hang on a second. I'm sure this is just another hoax. America today is not like the America of 2001. There is no 9/11 happening on our soil, ever again. I heard you were on leave so just relax for a day. I'm heading out to my office. I'll see if I can reach out to the President. You know he is busy with the North Korean President."

"Hoax or not, we need to take every threat very seriously. I'll worry about my vacation. At a bare minimum, we should begin checking all pickup trucks, box vans, and semi-trucks headed into the major cities. We should also consider shutting down the Metro."

"Which cities?"

"All the heavily populated cities, starting with New York, Washington—"

"Don't be stupid, Helms," Mattis interrupted him. "We can't just shut our cities without any credible intel."

. . .

"This is credible intel and an emergency. You need to tell the President that this is happening today, whether he likes it or not. If you want me in DC, I can arrive in an hour."

"No need Helms. I hear you, let me talk to the President. I'll call you back." Mattis didn't wait for Helms's response. It took Helms a few seconds to realize that Mattis had hung up on him. Was he really going to talk to the President? He decided it was better to deliver a summary report to Mattis just in case.

His phone rang. It was the FBI director. "Bill, I checked with my sources, there is no intel on any attack. Are you sure that your source is credible?"

"Yes, we need to dig harder."

Suddenly Helms's office door opened. It was Andrew. "Sir, you need to see this." He switched on the television.

The newscaster was hysterical. "A minute ago, two near-simultaneous explosions have been reported at Manhattan and Houston."

This was much worse than what Helms had estimated. The attacks had begun, and the world's most powerful nation wasn't the least bit prepared for it.

THE END.

—> GET WICKED BLOOD <—

SAM WICK UNIVERSE THRILLER #7

READ FIRST 3 CHAPTERS NEXT. TURN THE PAGE.

Thank you for reading my book. I hope you would have enjoyed it. Would you be interested in telling me your views on the story?

LEAVE A REVIEW - USA
LEAVE A REVIEW - UK
LEAVE A REVIEW - AUSTRALIA
LEAVE A REVIEW - CANADA
GOODREADS

Book reviews are not only important to you as a readers, but they are critically important to authors like me. As a novelist, I can tell you that I depend heavily on reviews from my readers.

They not only help others to find my books, but more importantly, they help me to improve my craft so the next book I write will be even better.

Well I am here to urge you, dear reader, to leave book reviews either on Amazon, Goodreads or BookBub.

Where you can write review on the Amazon book page

Click the links above and they will open the respective review pages of my book in your preferred Amazon store.

Click the button "Write a customer review" (Please note that the words might vary in your country's amazon store)

On clicking the button, you will be taken to a page where you can rate the book from 1 to 5 stars (5 being the highest) and you can write a couple of line about the book.

If you face any issues, please let me know at *chaseaustincreative@gmail.com* and I will be glad to help you with the process.

—> GET WICKED BLOOD <—

SAM WICK UNIVERSE THRILLER #7

ABOUT WICKED BLOOD

America is under attack and the world's most powerful nation isn't the least bit ready for it. **Can Sam Wick save his motherland?**

CHAPTER 1

0100 hours, a deserted airfield in Texas

"You've sinned, Mahfouz." Abdul Rahman Yasin's voice reverberated in the abandoned hangar. Standing on a platform, Yasin looked down on a young man in his late teens. The man was Otis but, in the camp, people knew him as Mahfouz, and Mahfouz was on trial for his sins. "You've violated the sacred pact between yourself and Allah. You have betrayed your brothers. You've broken their trust, but Allah is kind. He wants you to choose your own destiny. So, what will it be Mahfouz? What's your destiny?" Yasin's black eyes gazed at the impressionable young man.

"I deserve death."

Twenty-nine other young men in three straight lines watched Mahfouz choosing his destiny with a certain defiance.

.   .   .

"Speak to everyone about your sin." Yasin was the judge but the twenty-nine others were the jury.

"I broke the sacred pact when I asked one of my brothers about his family. The family that we have forsaken."

"Mahfouz, why did you do that?" Yasin's voice was pained.

Mahfouz remained silent.

Yasin looked at the sky and closed his eyes. "Inna lillahi wa inna ilayhi raji'un. (We belong to Allah and to Him we shall return)." He opened his eyes and observed his students. "Laqad han waqtuh. (His time has come.)" He spoke with a finality in his tone and twenty-nine pairs of feet moved towards Mahfouz.

Mahfouz turned around facing his executioners. In their eyes, he could see a multitude of emotions—hate, fear, shock, rejection...sympathy.

"La tuqaliq, Allah sayakun latif (Don't worry, Allah will be kind)," Mahfouz spoke to his executioners in Arabic. These boys were his brothers and he wanted them to be strong.

Shahrukh, who was closest to Mahfouz heard him speak and dealt the first blow. Mahfouz saw it coming and his natural instincts forced him to block it with both hands. "Forgive me." The two words immediately escaped his lips.

The first blow was the initiation. Body blows and kicks rained on him. He took them all without putting up a defense. But his young, vulnerable body could only take so much. He fell to the ground, but none of his executioners stopped.

Yasin remained on the platform watching Mahfouz being beaten to his death. His pupils had just passed the last stage of their six month-long training magnificently.   He now had twenty-nine merciless, trained soldiers who would do anything he wanted them to do. And today, he wanted the USA to burn.

Chapter 2

0150 hours

Yasin was in his private room, sitting on his knees, his hands placed flat on his thighs.

"O Allah, forgive me, have mercy on me, strengthen me, raise me in status, pardon me and grant me provision."

Shahrukh, a twenty-year-old young man and one of his star pupils, stood silently at the open door, waiting for Yasin to notice him. His eyes were alert, posture tense, gaze fixed on his commander. He didn't have the courage to interrupt Yasin during his Namaz. No one did.

"Subhanna rabbiyal a'laa. Subhanna rabbiyal a'laa. Subhanna rabbiyal a'laa." Yasin turned his head, first to his right and then left. He opened his eyes unhurriedly and noticed Shahrukh at the door, watching his every move like a loyal servant.

Yasin got to his feet and put on his slippers. He gave Shahrukh a nod to let him know he was ready. Shahrukh nodded in return and turned around to alert others.

Yasin smiled to himself, thinking of the fidelity Shahrukh and others had towards his words. From the day this had started, Yasin had vigorously sought boys like Shahrukh to be part of his army. Loyal to the core and impressionable. What they had lacked was training, and Yasin had polished them to be effective and efficient. Each one of them. Thirty in total. Now twenty-nine. Ready to plunge into anything with everything they had, at Yasin's word.

Today was the day to test their mettle.

Yasin replaced his kufi skullcap, worn during the Namaz, with a white Islamic turban. Military green fatigues completed his getup.

.   .   .

He left from his private room and entered a large space. The hangar of the deserted airfield was on the outskirts of Texas. No hum of traffic or buzz of streetlights. Just crickets. Companions Yasin didn't mind.

In fact, "hangar" was a very loose description for the space. It was more like a warehouse—high ceiling, cracked floor, rust eating away at the walls. The roller doors were up, and the entire structure seemed like it wouldn't take more than a slight breeze to collapse it. The building was illuminated with flickering overhead lights. Outside overgrown weeds snaked through the cracks. A field of dead grass stretched out in all directions revealing nothing but flat ground as far as the eye could see. But there was something else. Three Bell 205As and a Cessna sat outside, ready for take-off.

The air was lighter compared to the heaviness of the city, but it was still hot and wet. The night breeze failed to give any respite. Yasin sweltered in the heat, but he paid scant attention to it. He had seen worse.

He observed his mentees, waiting silently in three straight lines next to a makeshift platform at the far corner of the hangar, the very platform from which he had sentenced Mahfouz to death.

⊏⊐

Chapter 3

The cadets bowed their heads as Yasin walked up to the dais. He turned to face twenty-nine pair of eyes. His sleeves were rolled up, revealing muscular forearms. His face was thoughtful and intelligent, but it betrayed no emotion. A warrior's look was in his eyes. They all recognized the intensity—a mix of determination and ruthlessness.

For strangers, he was as normal as one would expect a person to be. He had a full head of thick black hair and a tanned face with a trimmed beard and a sharp mustache. People knew him as Ed McCarthy, a mild-mannered security guard at this deserted airfield, employed by an obscure North Dakota facilities management firm. On paper, his job was to take care of the airstrip and the hangar. The nearest town was fifteen miles to the north and he rarely visited it. Whenever he did, it was always for groceries, which were always paid for in cash. The cashier never looked at him twice. No one ever did.

Yasin had appeared in this town, seven months ago with three men. For the next thirty days, they had worked on creating makeshift living spaces for thirty more people, a soundproof space that covered one third of the hangar, a simulation room and a makeshift kitchen.

All this required cash. The money found its way to him through Irfan-Ul-Haq, aka the Great Cleric, a Pakistani religious leader with a shrewd expertise for diverting American aid sent to countries like Pakistan, Afghanistan and Iraq, for terrorist operations.

. . .

On the twenty-eighth day the three men left, leaving Yasin alone. Two days later the first lot of fifteen men arrived and three later, the next fifteen.

These were not some randomly selected trainees. They were recruited by Yasin based on their age, mixed parentage and citizenship. –They were all in their early twenties, had one Muslim parent and were American citizens with valid social security numbers. Some of them were from affluent families, several had parents who commanded wide respect in their communities, almost all had gone to good schools and been at the top of their class for most of their academic lives. But the most important thing they had in common was their extreme abhorrence for America's broken system.

And now they were going to spend the next six months of their lives on that airfield, right under the American government's nose, plotting the country's downfall.

Over six months, Yasin trained them in hand-to-hand combat, the use of different kinds of firearms—assault rifles, submachine guns and pistols—in the soundproof cabins. They learned to handle grenades and worked with every known kind of explosive. The training also covered a detailed lowdown of guerilla warfare and the deadly Palestinian terror strategies of deep insertion.

The target cities had already been identified. They were code-named Alpha, Beta and Gamma and broken down to their bare basics—subways, police station locations, sewer networks, train systems, electric grids, water supplies, government institutions, schools, malls, theatres. Weekly simulations augmented familiarity with the terrain. Mock battles in which different ground situations were replicated gave the young men a real feel of covering their bases quickly while taking care of any obstructions.

The cadets were given a new identity. None of them could ask anyone else about anything except what they were learning there. Talking about old identities or families or girlfriends or past life was forbidden; breaking this pact meant a death sentence. The mission was more important than small talk about one's past. All thirty of them had been reborn on that airfield.

The last stage of the training was to assess if they would hesitate to kill a fellow American and that was why, when Yasin came to know about Mahfouz's breach of trust, he waited till the last day of the training to order his death at the hands of his mates. By sacrificing Mahfouz, he had made sure that his six months of regimented training was successful in weeding out any vestige of humanity from every cadet's conscious. Now, not a shred of emotion or doubt would cloud their minds when the time came for them to kill.

Still Yasin knew that no training could prepare them to take on the FBI and the CIA and that's why the attacks were not aimed to seize control but to inflict maximum damage and then immediately withdraw to avoid retaliation. The assault's sole objective was "destroy and move".

. . .

America wouldn't even know what had hit her.

BUY WICKED BLOOD

(Sam Wick Universe Thriller #7)

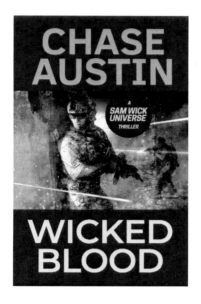

YOUR FREE BOOKS

Do not forget to download your FREE COPY of WICKED STORM & WICKED SHOT.

Click the link - www.thechaseaustin.com

DEDICATION

To My Boss

ACKNOWLEDGMENTS

A big thanks to **Deborah Rayment, Viett Hanh, Heather W., David C. Taylor, Stephen Gore, Jo Derooy, Kathryn M., Hope G., Francis P., Craig W. Carrier, Kaye G., Cath McTernan, Jane J, Jennifer, Sam Stokes,** and **Cynthia** for their helpful inputs on making the book precise and better.

To my **advance readers group** who are nothing but supportive of my writing and extremely helpful in rectifying mistakes that could have ruined the experience of reading this story.

ABOUT THE AUTHOR

Dear Fabulous Reader,

Thank you for reading. If you're a fan of Sam Wick, spread the word to friends, family, book clubs, and reader groups online.

I would love to hear from you. Let's connect @
www.thechaseaustin.com
chaseaustincreative@gmail.com

Join my Facebook group below to get behind the scene content or follow me on Goodreads, Instagram or BookBub.

Made in United States
North Haven, CT
23 December 2022

30077481R00114